Damien
The Vampeal

Tales of a gay witch
Skeletons in the Closet **(Available)**
In the Light of the Moon **(Available)**
Trapped in a House of Cards **(Coming soon)**

Damien the Devil:
Child Under the Stairs **(Available)**
Shattered Recollection **(Available)**
Keeper of the Forsaken **(Available)**

Curious Thing About The Apartment Vent: **(Available)**

Whispers of a perfect world **(Coming soon)**

Published by Noland Books.

Child Under the Stairs. Copyright © 2020
Shattered Recollection Copyright © 2022
Keeper of the Forsaken Copyright © 2024

Copyright © by Raymond Noland

All rights reserved. No part of this publication may be reproduced, stored, or transmitted in any form or by any means, electronic, mechanical, photocopying, recording, scanning, or otherwise, without written permission from the publisher. It is illegal to copy this book, post it on a website, or distribute it by any other means without permission.

Cover art by
SelfPubBookCovers.com/ DimitriElevit

Child Under The Stairs edited by Reedsy/ Donald Weise

Shattered Recollection and Keeper Of The Forsaken edited by Reedsy/Dominic Wakeford

Damien
The Vampeal

R. D. Noland

Child Under the Stairs

Damien the Devil

Book One

Chapter One
Damien

Throughout most of my young life, I always knew that I was different from the other children at the foster home, although the reason always escaped me. Now that I am fourteen and soon to be fifteen, I cannot stop staring at myself in the mirror. I find myself engrossed not in the typical teenage activities, but rather fixated on my now pearly white, retractable fangs, rather than the typical adolescent preoccupations with their changing bodies, hair, or acne.

A few years ago, one of my caseworkers sat me down and explained about my family and what I was. I knew about my mother's passing when I was born. Most of my life, I lived in foster care and had been bumped around from home to home. Periodically, I would have someone come to check on me, a so-called "guardian". One such guardian came to visit me following an incident at one of my foster homes involving a pain in the ass boy named Tommy.

His bullying towards me and the other children eventually led to a confrontation where, after a physical altercation, prompted me to defend myself. He threw a couple of punches at me and missed. Getting tired of this, I grabbed his arm after he tried to land another punch. In the heat of the moment, something extraordinary happened. I felt this horrible pain in my hand, but it was quickly replaced by this overwhelming surge of energy. Before I knew it, my nails grew, digging into the side of Tommy's arm, penetrating his flesh. I let go of Tommy as he collapsed, his eyes rolling back into his head as he hit the floor. I found myself baffled by what had happened; all I knew is that I felt different after that. A surge of energy heightened all my senses to an extraordinary degree that enabled me with newfound abilities. My sensory perceptions were heightened significantly. Sounds reverberated with clarity, my sense of smell intensified, and even the distant reading of a newspaper became possible. One of the other kids came in and called for help.

As everyone rushed in, Tommy collapsed on the floor. One of the foster parents asked me what had happened.

I found myself at a loss for words when questioned about the incident.

They told me to go to my room, and someone would come up to talk to me later. I watched as they left the house, taking Tommy to the hospital for a doctor to examine him.

About an hour later, there was a knock on the door. Mr. Osborne, my caseworker, entered my room. I could not look up at him; I knew that I was in trouble but was at a loss knowing exactly what I had done and why. Mr. Osborne approached me beside the bed.

Mr. Osborne asked, "How are you doing, William?"

I replied, "I am alright, I guess. Am I in trouble?"

He asked, "Why do you ask that, my boy?"

I told him what happened between Tommy and me, how he passed out when I touched him.

Mr. Osborne explained, " The doctor said Tommy will be okay. He passed out from exhaustion and will be fine in a few days of bed rest. No one knows what truly happened or who you are."

This caught me off guard, and I gave him a very curious look. "What the heck are you talking about?"

Mr. Osborne informed me that I was different from the other children in the house. He began to shed light on my true nature, revealing that I was a descendant of a vampire and a human, a halfling and that I was born of supernatural lineage known as a "Vampeal". He also disclosed his affiliation with the Feral Society, an organization that guides individuals with special abilities like mine in navigating society. In his organization, he is what you would call a "Renfield"; it is their responsibility to keep an eye on other children like me until they come of age.

Despite my initial skepticism, my reality began to dawn upon me. Mr. Osborne's story of my vampeal heritage, a hybrid offspring of a vampire mother and a human father, left me grappling with a tale that seemed lifted from some dusty old book. As I tried to process this information, doubts and disbelief clouded my mind, yet a growing sense of transformation stirred within me. But I still did not want to admit to myself that I was a freak or an abomination. I did not want the other children to treat me differently and think I was some kind of monster.

I confronted Mr. Osborne with a sharp tone. " Are you out of your mind? I am not different from any of the other kids."

"William, we are both aware that is not true. How did you feel after you injured Tommy's arm downstairs? There are small puncture marks on his arm that are barely visible because they heal almost instantly unless you know what you are looking for. Do not worry, no one else suspects anything, it is our little secret."

Feeling uneasy and agitated, I shook my head and moved to the other side of the room. I apologize for hurting him. " But what am I exactly?"

He explained, "As I told you before, you are what we refer to as a vampeal, yes you heard correctly. You are not a vampire, the so-called living-dead, but a blend of both. You were born, not turned. Your mother was a vampire who passed away giving birth to you. It is hard for a vampire to conceive a child let alone give birth to one, the Legends are true, but the folklore is not entirely accurate. "There are vampires, werewolves, witches, fairies, and many other mystical beings hidden in the shadows of this world."

I could not help but fidget as he told this story. It was overwhelming to process. Just over an hour ago, I thought these things were mere fairy tales, and now I was expected to believe they were true.

In a sarcastic tone, I inquired, "Will I start craving blood or burst into flames if I step out into the sunlight?"

Mr. Osborne began to laugh. "No, nothing of the sort. You possess a soul with a beating heart and a digestive system, allowing you to consume regular food. You can withstand sunlight, but I suspect that prolonged exposure may result in a severe sunburn. Your fangs will likely emerge around puberty, I think. However, you do not need to drink blood to survive. The fibers in your fingers under your nails absorb a person's life energy, granting you vampire-like abilities. Most individuals pass out long before any real harm is done. But you do have to be careful so no one finds out your true nature, as they may mistake you for a real vampire and attempt to harm you. You are still mortal and can die just like the rest of us, even though I think you can heal remarkably fast."

Trying to compose myself, I listened intently to Mr. Osborne's words and moved to sit on the adjacent bed, although I was still skeptical.

"How can I be certain that you are telling me the truth and not merely fabricating some story like some deranged old man?"

Once again, he just laughs " You should still have some residual life energy from the boy downstairs for a few hours, granting you enhanced speed, strength, and heightened senses. Feel free to test it out."

I reached for the brass bars on the headboard, astonished by how easily they bent. I sprinted across the room in the blink of an eye but failed to stop, crashing right into the wall and tumbling to the floor, Where I burst into laughter.

A voice called from downstairs, "IS EVERYTHING ALRIGHT UP THERE?"

Mr. Osborne reassured them, "YES, EVERYTHING IS FINE, WILLIAM SIMPLY STUMBLED."

"Are you convinced now, William? As you mature, your powers will strengthen. We will need to meet now that you are coming into your gifts. we will have to meet regularly to work on controlling your abilities."

That moment happened four years ago, spanning several foster homes. Following that, I adopted the nickname "Damien the Devil" from Tommy after he learned my middle name is Damien. I embraced it and then went by the name Damien Lampir. Despite the disapproval of my foster families, especially this religious one. I wondered why they would place me in such an environment, knowing my true nature. Rumor has it a new boy will be arriving tomorrow. As if being a vampeal was not challenging enough, I am now dealing with having new emotions towards other boys.

They scrutinize us incessantly, subjecting us to daily Bible readings. I am not sure how much more I can take from their discipline. Now with Mr. Osborne retiring, I must talk to the new Renfield to explore a more suitable solution.

Chapter Two
Pat

I am Patrick Davison accompanied by my twin brother, Matthew, we are sitting in an office, anticipating an interview. Interestingly, neither of us has pursued employment opportunities for quite some time. I recently completed my college education in 1979 and have since been self-employed part-time as a truck driver. While Matthew, who also works full-time as a truck driver, helped contribute to funding for my education. Now, it is Matthew's turn to pursue college, but both of us are open to seizing any promising opportunities that may arise.

I started to feel a bit uncomfortable as we waited for further instruction. The office had a somewhat shabby appearance, with green-painted walls and a floor of white and black checkerboard tiles. The receptionist, sporting cat-rimmed glasses, was seated behind an antiquated oak desk.

Finally, the receptionist informed us, " Mr. Craft will see you now."

We entered another office, not much different from the previous one, where we were greeted by a short, bald man with a face that resembled a bulldog and was smoking a cigar. He was only about five feet tall; he was a peculiar little man.

He approached us from behind the desk with a welcoming smile, " Ah, the Davison brothers, delighted to make your acquaintance. I am Mr. Craft, please take a seat. I presume you are curious as to why I summoned you here? I have a proposition for you gentlemen. We are seeking individuals with unique talents. You have captured our attention for some time now."

Mr. Craft retrieved a file from his desk and perused its contents, muttering to himself, "Let's see, Patrick attended Ohio State University, specializing in social work. You were involved in a relationship with Stephen Miller, now employed as a police officer, and you have been working part-time as a truck driver. Matthew also works as a truck driver, taking over the business after your father's health setback. No notable relationship to speak of. Ah, there it is."

Turning towards the bookcase on the right, Mr. Craft beckoned, "Betty, could you join us?"

Initially assuming he was summoning the receptionist from the front office, I soon detected the soft hum of approaching footsteps.

Matthew leaned over and whispered to me, "It appears a lady is emerging from the bookcase."

I turned around and scanned the room, only to find Mr. Craft in sight. However, a faint humming sound persisted, giving me the eerie sensation that a ghostly presence loomed.

Turning my head slightly to the side to hear her better. "Hello, you must be Betty?"

She ceased her humming and responded in a soft, melodic voice, "Yes, Patrick, you can hear me, and I noticed that your brother can see me."

I relayed Betty's words to Mat.

He acknowledged, "Yes, Ma'am, I can see you."

Mr. Craft addressed her. "That will be all for now, Betty."

She giggled lightly and faded back into the bookcase.

Mr. Craft closed the file. "Sorry gentleman, I needed to confirm the accuracy of the report firsthand. As I was saying, we are seeking individuals with unique abilities."

Matt inquired, "You are searching for truck drivers who can see spirits?"

The man laughed. "No, not quite. We are looking for someone who possesses a connection to the supernatural. I represent the organization known as the Feral Society. We have numerous offices situated across the globe, with a number of agents with many unique talents. Our primary focus lies in mentoring supernatural children and assisting them in integrating into society. Upon reaching adulthood, many choose to join our organization, where we tackle challenges that the local authorities are unable to resolve. Should either of you accept the position, I have specific assignments lined up for both of you. Patrick, I have a young man here in Cincinnati who requires your mentorship, while Matthew, I have an assignment for you at a university in Florida. Your expertise in truck driving would serve as an excellent cover for your activities. The compensation offered is quite substantial. So, gentlemen, what is your decision? Are you in or out?"

I asked Mr. Craft, "May I have a brief moment to discuss it over with Matt?"

Mr. Craft nodded in agreement, allowing us some time to deliberate between ourselves. Mr. Craft proceeded to the adjacent office to speak with his receptionist.

I turned to Matt and questioned, "What are your thoughts on this matter?"

Matt paused, placing his hand on his chin to consider. "This could be a good opportunity, as long as it does not involve any illegal activities. Perhaps I could enroll in some courses at the University?"

I agreed, "This experience could indeed be an exciting adventure for both of us."

I then informed the receptionist that we have come to a decision. Mr. Craft returned to the office. "We are in agreement with your proposal, provided there are no illegal activities."

The bulldog smiled and clapped his hands together. "Excellent, gentlemen, let's finalize the necessary documents."

He proceeded to the bookcase from which the ghost had recently emerged. Tugging on a book, he revealed a hidden passageway. I looked at Matt in astonishment as we followed behind Mr. Craft into the hallway.

He turned to us and remarked, "This area serves as the primary hub of operations within this office."

Glancing around, I observed numerous elegant offices that bore no resemblance to the modest one we had departed. The decor included wallpaper, antique Renaissance paintings, and Art Deco wall sconces illuminating the way. Eventually, we arrived at another lavishly furnished office at the end of the hallway. The office boasted black leather chairs and a mahogany desk adorned with rows and rows of books.

Mr. Craft settled behind the desk and gestured, " Please take a seat, gentlemen. What knowledge do you have regarding vampires, werewolves, and witches?"

I shrugged, "Are you suggesting they exist? My only knowledge is based on what we've read in books and seen in movies."

The bulldog raised an eyebrow and let out a bark in response. "So you believe in ghosts, but not other supernatural beings. Indeed they are real. However, the accuracy of the legends surrounding them has changed over time. We can delve deeper into that topic at a more suitable time"

Mr. Craft passed a book to each of us with the title "Mystical Creatures" displayed prominently on the cover.

Mr. Craft explained, "This book serves as a comprehensive compilation of various creatures known to exist. Patrick, your charge is a young man named Damien Lampir, a vampeal, half human, half vampire, at the age of fourteen, who has experienced a tumultuous childhood in various foster homes. Matthew, your responsibility is a sixteen-year-old attending the university in Florida. I have the necessary contract for both of you to sign if you're interested, and then we can proceed."

Chapter Three
Damien

I looked out the window in anticipation to catch a glimpse of the new boy that social services were to bring today. As I rested on my bed, I found myself with little to occupy my time around here. The foster mother, a devout follower of the Bible, perceives everything as evil and affiliated with Satan. I cannot help but wonder who orchestrated this cruel joke, placing me in a place like this.

As I heard the sound of a car approaching outside, I hurried to the bedroom window. Then I spotted a tall, slender, blonde- haired boy, who appeared to be around sixteen years old getting out of a black mid-sized vehicle. After engaging in a conversation with our foster mother at the front entrance, He eventually glanced up at the window where I stood, causing me to momentarily back away. With a mischievous grin, he made his way towards the house, prompting me to eavesdrop on their conversation as they paused by the staircase just slightly within my view. Once more, the blonde-haired boy looked up in my direction.

I overheard Mrs. Crabtree invite him to the study, to which he gave me a playful wink before entering the room.

My heart fluttered in surprise. "Wait! Did a boy just? No, it cannot be."

Then I heard footsteps coming from the study as they headed up the stairs. Hastily, I sprinted and leaped onto the bedroom. Mrs. Crabtree escorted the blonde-haired boy into the room.

She addressed Brian, "you will be sharing this room with this individual known as Damien. Damien this is Brian, you are both to adhere to a set of rules. Lights out promptly at eight, do not forget to read the Bible, and say your prayers before retiring for the night. Dinner is served at five o'clock, and all the children are expected to assist in the preparation and cleanup of the kitchen. Access to the girls' room is prohibited. Furthermore, Damien, refrain from influencing Brian with any improper ideas. I shall summon you for dinner. Have a good day, gentlemen."

Mrs. Crabtree proceeded downstairs and entered the living room. Brian turned to me. "What did she mean by improper ideas?"

I looked away, "she perceives me as the devil, attempting to lead others astray and take everyone to hell with me."

He laughed. "Well that sounds amusing. I doubt there will be much fun with her around. Perhaps we should paint our nails black and apply some eyeliner. I believe that would certainly drive her crazy."

I thought to myself, *if I truly wanted to drive her crazy, I could simply reveal my fangs. However, it might also freak Brian out as well.*

I simply chuckled. " You may be right."

I observed Brian rummaging through his belongings, engaging in light conversation. I must admit that he is a very handsome young man, somewhat skinny, but that can be improved upon. Then we heard the lady of the house summon us to prepare dinner. All the kids gathered in the dining room, where she assigned tasks for everyone. Brian and I were given the job of cleaning and peeling potatoes and carrots.

Once all of the chores were completed, she instructed us to go wash up and she will call everyone when dinner is ready. Each child took their turn washing up. As Brian and I changed our shirts, I glanced at his bare chest. When he turned towards me, I quickly turned away. Mrs. Crabtree summoned us for dinner, and we all proceeded to the dining room table. Brian and I deliberately sat at the opposite end of the table to distance ourselves as much as possible from Mrs. Crabtree.

I nudged Brian." You need to grab your food quickly when there are eight children present."

The foster mother instructed Brian to lead us in saying grace before we commenced our meal. When he was finished, we all dug into our food.

After the prayer, we eagerly began eating. I politely asked Brian, "Could you pass the rolls?" He graciously passed them to me. As he handed me the rolls, I could not help but notice his leg lightly brushed against mine. I stole a glance at him, then turning when feeling my cheeks flush with embarrassment, *could I be imagining that he was flirting with me? No, he is older than me; he probably views me as just a silly kid.*

When everyone had finished eating and it was time to clean up, Brian and I took charge of washing the dishes. He handled the washing while I focused on drying. We joked around and playfully splashed each other, making the chore more enjoyable. Although I typically hate doing dishes, Brian company made it bearable. with the other children already done and up in their rooms, we eventually finished the dishes and joined them upstairs.

Mrs. Crabtree intercepted us. "Do not forget to read the scripture and say your prayers before going to bed this evening." She advised.

"We will." We assured her before retiring to our room.

With the door closed, Brian turned to me, expressing his disbelief at Mrs. Crabtree's ridiculous demands. "Is she for real? Does she think we are both mere juveniles? The notion of saying your prayers seems rather old-fashioned, don't you agree?"

I sat on my bed. " Although I have not been here too long, it is vitally important to take Mrs. Crabtree's words seriously. Failing to do so might result in severe consequences, as she can exhibit a rather sadistic side when she wants to."

I could see Brian's disapproval on his face. "You are not kidding."

In response. "I wish I were joking, but I would be surprised if she decided to lock someone in the attic."

Brian giggled, "Well, that seems interesting. I kinda like playing in the attics. I have always had this dream of exploring a vast attic filled with valuable antiques that I can rummage through."

I simply shook my head. "You are definitely going to be trouble, I can see it now."

Mrs. Crabtree appeared at the doorway. "Shall we commence with our reading?"

In unison, we both responded, "Yes, Mrs. Crabtree."

Following her instructions, we changed into our pajamas and turned off the lights before getting into our beds. Despite my best efforts, I could not sleep as thoughts of Brian continued to occupy my mind.

Brian (whispered), "Damien, are you awake?"

I let out a sigh and (whispered), "Yeah, I can not sleep either."

So we both set upright on our beds. I gestured for silence by placing my finger up to my lips and whispered. "Shh, be quiet so she does not hear us."

Brian motioned for me to join him on his bed, and I agreed, bringing my blanket along.

I asked Brian inquisitively. "What brought you to this godforsaken place?

He softly giggled, responding. "You make it sound as though it is a prison."

I smiled in return. "Just wait, you may come to see it the same way. I lost my mother in childbirth and have never known who my father was. All the information about me is inaccessible until I reach the age of eighteen, as my records are sealed."

Brian offers his condolences. "Damien, it must have been hard for you."

I shrugged nonchalantly. "Mostly, it has not been too difficult. This marks my sixth home. However, Bible Betty has not made this placement welcoming. she has hated me ever since I got here. What about yourself?"

Brian shared his own story, "I lost my entire family in a plane crash while they were on holiday. I was unable to go because I got the flu, which made me stay home with my grandmother. I lived with her until she suffered a stroke and passed away. I have a trust fund, but I am unable to access it until I turn eighteen."

Turning to Brian."Now I am the one that is sorry. It seems that all the children here have a similar story; otherwise, they would not be here."

As I laid my head back and looked at Brian, the sole source of light in the room came from the street, casting a bluish hue on his face.

Directing his attention towards me, Brian remarked, "You know, you may be slightly younger but you seem to be nearly as mature as me. you are almost as tall as me, and you are more physically developed than I am."

Brian's words caused me to blush, a reaction I rarely exhibit. That's when I said the first thing that came to mind, "Thank you, I guess it is all in the genes."

My response made me feel stupid afterwards. Uncertain of my own behavior, I was overwhelmed by a sense of how hot I felt next to Brian, my palms were sweaty, and my stomach was churning. *"pull yourself together, Damien,"* I was afraid that Brian would perceive me as a mere child. Perhaps I should divert the conversation before I make a complete fool of myself. I straightened up and looked over at Brian. "Well, I wish we did not have school tomorrow, we could go down by the river. I like to go there when I want to get away and think, when Mrs. Crabtree gets too much."

Brian smiled. "Do not worry, you can show me later. This is your first year at this high school, right? It is my first year at this school as well, so it looks like it is both our first year in a new school together."

I told Brian, "Yep, I moved around a lot over the years and went to many schools. It always sucks when you have to start over again, making new friends. It's hard to get close to anyone, and they kinda look at you funny when they find out you're an orphan. They whisper behind your back, 'you are one of those kids.' So we tend to stay close to our own kind."

Brian confessed, "When mom and dad died, I didn't have to go to another school. My grandmother inherited the house, and I lived with her until she passed away." The house will go to me after I'm eighteen.

So I will be a ward of the state until then. But I'm glad I have already made at least one new friend already."

I nodded to Brian. "I'm happy you're here too. But I think we should try to get some sleep before school tomorrow."

It took considerable effort for me to return to my own bed. Although I wanted to sleep next to Brian, I was aware that such an action would not be well-received by the woman residing below. Consequently, I quietly made my way back to my own bed, where I lay gazing at the wall until sleep eventually overtook me.

Chapter Four
Damien

Brian and I got up early the following morning, preparing ourselves for the school day ahead. We carefully laid out our clothes on the bed, anticipating a quick change after breakfast. As we headed down to the kitchen, we were greeted by Mrs. Crabtree who had already set out bowls of steaming oatmeal for us and the other children. for all the kids. The younger kids eagerly arranged the spoons around the table, while I got out the glasses. I asked Brian to get the milk from the refrigerator. Mrs. Crabtree then placed a plate of toast, accompanied by a few sticks of margarine. The children promptly seated themselves and quickly devoured their breakfast within a few minutes. Once finished, we carefully disposed of our bowls and glasses in the sink. The eldest among us took charge of tidying up the kitchen and washing the dishes, before we all washed up and dressed for school. It was the responsibility of the older kids to ensure that the younger ones were properly dressed and ready for the school day. Given our close proximity to both the high school and the elementary school, just a few blocks away, we had to walk the younger children to their respective schools.

Mrs. Crabtree would not usually come with us in the morning, but she had to get Brian enrolled in high school. Therefore, Brian and Mrs. Crabtree proceeded to the principal's office. After saying goodbye to everyone, I made my way to my first class.

Mathematics was my first period subject, and I generally did well in it. However, on this particular day, I found it challenging to maintain my focus on my studies. I was primarily concerned about how Brian was doing on his first day. Anticipation for the class to end was killing me, yet I also was contemplating how I could skip my class, fixating on the clock and its relentless ticking of the second hand. Eventually, I finally gave in and decided to complete my class assignment, quickly finished all my math problems, and submitted my work to the teacher just as the bell rang. Swiftly I grabbed my books and proceeded to the hallway, retrieving my textbook for my next class from my locker. It was at that moment that I ran into Brian. Trying to conceal my delight at his presence, I maintained my excitement.

Brian leaned over and said."Let's ditch the rest of our classes. The weather is great, and I am not ready for this. Come on, let us get out of here."

I paused momentarily, and then I smiled. Casually, I returned my books to the locker and pivoted towards him. "Well, I have been thinking about leaving myself," I remarked.

Quickly we made our way to the exit, with Brian already making it out. However, just as I reached the door, a hand grasped my arm halting my departure. As I turned, it was none other than Principal Burns.

With a disapproving tone, he inquired. "Mr. Lampir, where do you think you are going?"

Glancing back at Brian, who urged me to hurry up, I turned back to face Principal Burns. With a swift movement, I gently touched his arm. I drained some of his life force, just enough to influence him to do as I suggest. "

I told Principal Burns firmly. "Brian is not feeling well; I am taking him home. Kindly excuse us both from our classes for the remainder of the day."

Acknowledging my request, Principal Burns repeated, "You both are excused from your class today. Take Brian home."

I released Principal Burns' arm and dashed out the door to meet up with Brian.

"Now that we've left, what do you want to do?"

"Didn't you mention that you wanted to show me the river?"

I nodded in agreement, and we made our way to the Ohio River. Brian and I strolled to the edge and looked out over the water.

"I appreciate the view from here. I can understand why it appeals to you." Brian remarked.

I turned towards him. "I find the view quite spectacular today as well."

With a mischievous grin, I lightly pushed him, causing him to lose his balance, and then took off running. Brian chased after me, and we eventually reached a bench. I maneuvered to the opposite side, placing the bench between us. Both of us paused for a moment to catch our breath, with me deliberately holding back so as not to get too far ahead. I could not resist teasing him, mocking him for being so slow. He laughed, and we resumed the chase again, circling around to the other side of the bench before stopping once more as I moved to the front.

Brian grinned. "Are you going to let me catch you, or shall we continue this playful pursuit all day?"

I laughed in response. "It would not be as enjoyable if I made it too easy for you, now would it?"

We circled back for a second round. During this time, I faked a stumble, as if I twisted my ankle and tumbled onto the grass.

Brian was concerned and rushed over to my side. "Damien, are you alright, did you hurt yourself?"

With the agility of a cat, I swiftly maneuvered and turned, tackling Brian to the ground before mounting him to restrain him.

A grin crossed my face. "I find it much more enjoyable to catch you, even if you were unaware of being pursued."

Leaning in closer to him, I paused mere inches from his face before grabbing his side and initiating a playful tickle attack. Brian erupted in laughter and squirmed frantically in an attempt to break free from my grasp. Both of us were consumed by laughter, to the point our sides were aching. Eventually, we collapsed on the ground beside each other, and after a few minutes, we regained our composure and sat upright. We had failed to notice that there were people passing by us, staring, and I was not sure in a good way.

Rising to my feet, I extended a hand to Brian. "We ought to move on."

We strolled further along the riverbank until we reached a park. Along the way, we passed a variety of people, including joggers, skaters, and a woman feeding the pigeons.

Suddenly, Brian turned to me and suggested, "Considering there are a lot of people out today, perhaps we should go somewhere that is a little more private."

I looked at him with a hint of suspicion. "What do you have in mind?"

Brian responded with a mischievous smile. " Remember our conversation about the attic last night? We could hide up there since we have some time to kill."

After a moment of consideration, I agreed. "We could enter through the rear of the house; there are windows that will not latch, we just need to climb up."

" Let's go." Brian urged.

And with that, we made our way to the back of the house, attempting to be very quiet. Scaling the trellis, we reached a small balcony adjacent to the window. Despite our best efforts to be discreet, Brian' foot became wedged in the window, nearly causing him to stumble. I swiftly managed to grab him, pulling him to safety. Once inside, I settled on the sofa while Brian moved towards an old rocking chair, which I promptly warned him against due to its loud creaking.

He muttered. "Alright, my apologies."

Brian then perched on the arm of the sofa. In the moment of silence, with both of us unsure of what to say, I sensed a tinge of anxiety in the air.

However, after a few seconds, Brian finally took the initiative and inquired, "Do you feel a bit warm? We have been quite active today, and I, for one, am feeling rather overheated."

Afterward, he removed his shirt and placed it on the sofa. My eyes widened as he stood there, only in his jeans, exposing his bare chest. After a moment of thought, I made a decision with a sense of boldness and determination. I followed suit and removed my shirt as well. Then we both reclined on the sofa.

"Damien, let us designate this as our special place, known only to us. We can come up here and talk about stuff that is private that we do not want anyone to know about."

I agreed, yet I found it challenging to focus on the conversation initially, as my attention was captivated by the sight of several beads of sweat trickling down Brian's chest. I regained my composure upon realizing that he caught me looking at him. Feeling embarrassed, I had to look away.

"Damien, have you ever met someone that you liked as a special friend, like in a romantic way?"

"No, I have not stayed in one place long enough to get emotionally attached to anyone. Have you met anyone special, Brian?"

I gazed up at Brian as he said, "There were a couple of boys whom I admired growing up."

I rose from my seat and approached the window, still feeling a bit nervous. "So do you prefer boys?"

Then he revealed to me. "Yes, I believe you also have similar feelings as well. I have observed the way you look at me when you think I am not looking. Do not worry, I feel the same way for you."

I turned around and expressed, "I do not know, I have never had a kiss with anyone, and someone like Mrs. Crabtree feels that it is inappropriate for two guys to have romantic feelings for each other."

Brian approached the window and gently traced his fingers from my arm to my chest, catching a droplet of sweat along the way.

He grinned, "It is alright if you are not sure how you feel. I simply wanted you to know, I like you."

I felt a wave of relief wash over me, yet a twinge of fear still lingered. These emotions were entirely new to me, let alone somebody returning them.

Glancing at my watch, I remarked, "We need to leave now to pick up the kids from the elementary school, as we usually do."

Afterward, Brian and I grabbed our shirts and climbed back out the window, descending down the trellis. Quietly, we snuck through the back to avoid Mrs. Crabtree detection. Reuniting with the other kids without attention, we resumed our activities as if nothing had happened. Upon returning home, we engaged in our daily dull routine of chores, washing up, and preparing for dinner. Brian's company brought a delightful touch of entertainment to the evening.

As bedtime approached, we changed into our pajamas. I still had a hard time falling asleep, as my mind replayed the events of the wonderful day and conversations I had with Brian. While I did have feelings for boys, I was too afraid to acknowledge them to myself.

Brian's voice broke the silence once more, inquiring, "Are you awake?"

I turned towards him and replied. "Yeah, I am still awake."

Brian sat upright and gestured for me to come over, prompting me to move to his bed once more.

I whispered to him. "I have been thinking about what we talked about earlier today, and you are correct. Indeed, I do like boys, including yourself. However, I am afraid because for the first time in a long time, I do not know what to do or handle it. I have always had to stay strong, regardless of the circumstances."

Brian put his arms around me in a comforting embrace. "Sometimes, you just have to trust that someone will be there for you, and you do not have to be on your own forever."

I was still too embarrassed to look at him. Finally, when I did, Brian leaned over to me and gently caressed my cheek with his finger. As his face drew near to mine, he turned his head slightly, and I did the same, and our lips met. I put my arms around him, closed my eyes, and he did the same as we kissed for the very first time. However, the moment was suddenly shattered as Mrs. Crabtree burst into the room and turned on the lights.

She had a look of disgust on her face. "I knew of your malevolent nature, Damien, yet I never fathomed… This transgression is the epitome of your depravity, attempting to entice the newcomer into your sinful ways. Your principal just called about Brian's well-being, as it seems that both of you skipped most of your classes today. Is this the activity you two were engaging in behind my back?"

We both leaped off the bed. Then Brian stated, "Damien came over to my bed, and it was he who initiated the kiss."

I turned to him with a mixture of disdain and disbelief as I struggled to come to terms with his betrayal in light of our previous discussions.

Then the old crone proceeded to the door. "I demand that you immediately leave my house this evening! I refuse to remain here under my roof with the children!"

Brian attempted to interject with Mrs. Crabtree, she was not receptive. She instructed him to go downstairs. Brian pushed past her, and she slammed the door behind him. I changed my clothes, then proceeded to gather some of my things and put them in my backpack. Tears started to well up in my eyes, yet I had to suppress them. I do not want Mrs. Crabtree to have the satisfaction of seeing me like this. The new Renfield was starting soon, so I will come back and get the rest of the stuff later. I went downstairs to find the children crying, pleading for me to stay. Mrs. Crabtree sternly reprimanded the children to stop and get away from me. She proceeded towards the front door and swung it open.

Observing the children standing behind me, I reassured them, "Everything will be fine."

I glared at Brian, and he looked away. Then I turned back towards Mrs. Crabtree, revealing my fangs and emitting a low growl. Startled, she stumbled backwards, falling to the floor while shielding her face with her arms and emitting a shrill shriek. With a sinister smirk, I exited through the door.

Chapter Five

Pat

Mr. Craft placed a pen on top of the contracts. "Gentleman, kindly add your signatures on the dotted line, and we will get started. Just be grateful that we do not practice signing in blood anymore." He remarked with a chuckle. "Relax, gentlemen, I am joking, of course; we never truly observed that custom."

Matt and I promptly signed the documents and passed them to Mr. Craft. A warm smile graced Mr. Craft's face. "Excellent gentleman, Matthew, would you please proceed to the office door where you will find my receptionist, Miss Periwinkle? She will provide you with the necessary information for your assignment."

Matt nodded in acknowledgment and made his way to the neighboring office.

Returning his attention to me, Mr. Craft handed me a file pertaining to Damien. "Patrick, I urge you to read this document tonight. Tomorrow, you are to visit the foster home where Damien is currently staying. It appears that an error has been made in his placement; the foster mother is an overzealous Bible advocate... well, you understand. We may need to take action in relocating Damien to a new home. Go check on your brother and provide me with a report tomorrow following your meeting with Damien."

I expressed my gratitude to Mr. Craft for granting us this opportunity. After shaking Mr. Craft's hand, I proceeded to the adjacent office to check on Matt. As I reached for the door handle, Matt emerged from the office with a smile. We exited the building, got into the truck, and headed home.

I asked Matt, "What assignment did Mr. Craft give you?"

He laughed, "I am assigned to oversee a sixteen-year-old exceptional individual of human/dwarf descent who is currently in his third year of college. I will be flying to Florida tomorrow, and in first-class no less!"

I responded, "Impressive indeed. First-class accommodations on the first day. I am scheduled to meet my assigned ward tomorrow, a fourteen-year-old individual of human/vampire heritage." I must review his dossier this evening."

Upon our return home, Matt prepared a meal while I retried to the study where I opened Damien's extensive file, as he has been within the system for an extended period. I thanked Matt for making us some sandwiches, placing them on the desk before exiting the room. Damien, for the most part, displayed commendable behavior. However, there were some issues with an individual in the past when he first manifested his extraordinary abilities. That led to the nickname "Damien the Devil." Nonetheless, it appears that the majority of the children hold him in high regard, with Damien assuming a protective role like a big brother.

There exists another dossier pertaining to the organization itself. It appears that all the legends are rooted in truth, although they got muddied over the ages. The world is still home to hundreds of thousands of mythical creatures, yet their populations have declined over the years due to intermingling with their human counterparts. This intermingling has resulted in the creation of hybrid offspring known as halflings. However, this development has not gone unnoticed by the supernatural and human realms, leading to conflict. Therefore, the Feral Society was established to maintain balance between the three worlds.

Upon entering the study, Matt inquired, "Do you have any idea what time it is?"

Glancing at the clock, I responded, "*Wow*, I was just getting into the documents provided by Mr. Craft. It is fascinating to uncover this vast unknown world that we had no idea existed. Perhaps our exposure to spirits throughout our lives is why we did not freak out, having been pronounced dead at birth by the doctor when we were born. It took doctors approximately a minute to resuscitate us both. It was a hard delivery for our mother, having to undergo a C-section due to the umbilical cord being entwined around our necks, obstructing our oxygen supply. Matt, what is it like when you see a ghost?

He pondered for a moment. "I have never given it much thought, but if I had to characterize what I have seen, they appear mostly transparent. It is as though a mist is gliding along in a human form. Often, there is a lingering trail of mist trailing behind them. Their appearance can vary in color. Their emotions can shift rapidly. If the spirit is enraged and filled with hate, it appears as though it is engulfed in flames. However, the most terrifying manifestations are manifestations of pure malevolence. They are dark as coal and seem to drain the life from the room. So, Pat, what is your experience hearing them?"

I also hesitated for a second. "You are correct, we have never really discussed what it was like." We have never had cause to articulate it until now. It is not like conversing with a person in a regular manner; their voice reverberates and resonates. They can speak softly like a whisper or so deafening that it could knock you right off your feet if they're agitated. Now that I am back, I wish we had more time together before you have to run off. I missed you, bro."

Matt agreed. "I know, now it is my turn to run off to college in Florida." However, look at it this way, you should be able to have some kick-ass vacations in the warm sun when you come down to visit me."

I rose out of the chair and approached Matt, embracing him warmly and giving him a reassuring pat on the back. I informed Matt. "You make a valid point, that does sound like a delightful prospect. Nevertheless, I believe it is time to retire for the night as you pointed out, it is quite late."

Chapter Six
Damien

Alright, Damien. What predicament have you gotten yourself into this time? Where am I going to go at this time of night? I knew that woman was going to be trouble, and I really wanted to get back at her for what she had done. I could have ripped her apart, but that would only make me a monster; then I would have lived up to the nickname that Tommy gave me. It would have been awful to subject the children to such a nightmare. But I am glad to be out of that house and far away from her.

Surveying my surroundings, pondering my current location. Well, I am facing towards the river. Perhaps heading down there to clear my head might be helpful. I should contact my Renfield tomorrow and tell him of the situation. I am curious as to who the new guardian will be?

After reaching the riverbank and looking across to the Kentucky side, I love how it looks at night, with the shimmering lights dancing on the water surface. Feeling a slight chill from the river breeze, I put on my jacket and strolled along the edge, encountering a few passersby.

There was a couple sharing a tender moment on the park bench that reminded me of the kiss I shared with Brian, shattered by an unwelcome interruption. How could Brian lie and accuse me of instigating it? Tonight was my first kiss with anyone.

Continuing to walk along the river, I heard approaching footsteps. Glancing back, I noticed a man in a lengthy overcoat. Stepping aside near the railing, I allowed him to pass before resuming my observation of the water, admiring the enchanting view of the bridges illuminated against the spectacular night sky. Lost in thought as I kept going over all that had happened tonight, but then I was startled when the man doubled back unexpectedly. I cursed myself for not staying alert.

The man inquired, "Are you alright?"

Well, my trust in people was pretty much shattered tonight, even if he was just trying to be nice.

"Thank you, but I am fine." I replied.

He placed his hand on my shoulder and offered, "I have a nice warm place for you to spend the night, and if you are hungry I can make you something to eat. All I ask in return is that you be nice to me for a while, and we can have a little fun."

I turned towards him, removed his hand from my shoulder, and firmly repeated, "I have previously told you I am not interested!"

I began to walk away, but he grabbed my arm. This was not the night to piss me off. Therefore, I increased my grip on his arm, draining his energy as he grew weary and fell to his knees, his pupils dilated. With my influence, I compelled him to do as I instructed.

I informed him. "You felt genuinely concerned about my safety and well-being and wish to assist me for my misfortune, you will walk away and forget that we had this little conversation and locate the nearest police officer, and approach them and expose yourself to them."

I released my grasp on him, allowing him a moment to recover. Then I assisted him to his feet.

He asked. "What happened?"

I responded, "I was explaining what a rotten night I was having when you suddenly felt a little lightheaded. "I suggest you take a seat on the bench for a few minutes."

Expressing his gratitude, he stated. "I appreciate your help. I would like to offer you something as a token of my appreciation. Please help me over to the bench so I may rest for a second."

He pulled his wallet from his pocket and extracted a thick bundle of twenty-dollar bills, handing me a few before tucking the remainder back into his wallet. "You should go home right away, it is probably not very safe around here at night." He advised.

In response. I expressed my gratitude and assured him that I would go home just like he suggested and that he should take a break before heading home himself. With that, I walked away. I shuddered as a feeling of revulsion came over me when I realized the perv had touched me with inappropriate attention.

Upon reaching the park, I decided to sit down and figure out my next step. Fortunately, I have some money to hold me over for a few days. I still need to find a secure temporary place to stay until I can reach someone to let them know what happened. Suddenly, I got a feeling that someone else was watching me. Carefully, I scanned my surroundings, determined not to be caught off guard for a second time tonight. Although no one was in sight, I remained convinced that I was being watched. My attention was drawn upwards as a silhouette caught my attention amidst the trees. A faint odor of decay reached my heightened senses of smell. Sensing it was time to move on, I attempted to move forward, only to be obstructed by someone who dropped right in front of me. To my surprise, I found myself face to face with a young man with long red hair. No, not a man, but a vampire. Crouched like a frog, it fixed its gaze upon me, then rose upright and tilted its head to the side. Baring its fangs, it emitted a menacing hiss. In response, I returned the favor by exposing my own fangs in a defiant display.

Then it addressed me. "You have disturbed my dinner. As a result, you piqued my interest, little fang."

I responded, "What are you talking about, the perv that I left back there? Your dinner messed with me first, as you probably witnessed. and why in the hell did you just call me little fang?"

It emitted a low, menacing growl. "Because you are a halfling and your fangs will never fully develop; they are useless."

I chuckled softly. "I beg to differ." I shifted to the side, yet the vampire mirrored my movement.

The vampire inhaled deeply, then licked his lips and remarked. "I am curious about what your blood tastes like."

The vampire made a sudden lunge towards me, moving with remarkable agility. However, having recently fed, and luckily that it had not. I was slightly quicker and managed to seize its throat, exerting immediate pressure. It hissed and growled, yet as I was swiftly depleting its energy. Its skin darkened, flaked, and peeled. The creature attempted to strike at me, but I imminently grabbed his arm and effortlessly snapped it like a twig. It screamed in agony as I tossed the vampire aside as if it were a mere rag doll. It twisted and contorted in midair before landing back on its feet as if it were a cat.

He grabbed his arm tightly and hissed again. "This is not over little fang." Then the vampire darted off into the night.

I let out a sigh. "Why can't people just leave me be?"

It was then I noticed something strange. My vision seems distorted, the darkness of the night felt less intense, and the colors appeared brighter. I went over to the edge of the river and looked at my reflection. My eyes had changed color, now a luminous yellow resembling that of a wild creature. *"Well, this is certainly unexpected. I thought.*

Standing upright, I heard the rumble of thunder, and the wind was starting to whip up.

I stood there, looking at the sky. "Just great, I could have done without the rain, thank you." I muttered.

Realizing I needed to find shelter for the night, I sprinted away; my speed was almost miraculous. In a matter of moments, I found myself several blocks away from the river. Eventually, I finally stopped in an area with some abandoned warehouses. I found one hidden out of the way. I went around the side, and there was a door down a flight of stairs. The inscription on the door read "Magnolia Emporium." I pulled on the handle, twisted it, and snapped the lock. Just in time, I slipped inside as the rain began to pour down. Closing the door behind me, I made my way into the storeroom. Covered with white sheets, various items filled the space. I removed a few sheets, revealing an assortment of furniture. There was a cabinet near the door, which I pushed to block the entrance. Seating myself on a sofa, I bunched up some sheets to fashion a makeshift pillow, then laid down to finally get some rest.

Chapter Seven

Pat

I arrived at the Crabtree residence where Damien is currently staying. My stomach felt slightly uneasy, prompting me to take a few deep breaths to steady myself. As I embarked on my first day in the field, I did not know what to expect regarding what Damien and the foster family had in store. Today I have to make an evaluation as to whether this is the right environment for him to stay.

Approaching the door, I knocked, but there was no response. I repeated the action with more force, only to be greeted by a young girl, approximately ten years old, sporting pigtails.

Bending down slightly, I introduced myself, "Hello, I am here from Social Services to see Mrs. Crabtree."

The young girl graciously stepped aside to allow me in before closing the door behind us. She hastily ran off, yelling, "Mrs. Crabtree! There is a man here to see you."

Soon after, a middle-aged woman with a stern appearance, hair neatly coiled in a bun, and wearing a floral apron emerged from the back of the house, presumably from the kitchen.

As she dried her hands on the apron, she inquired, "How may I help you?"

I extended my hand in greeting, only she denied the gesture. "I am Mr. Davison, from Social Services. I have come to see one of your children. Could you have Damien join us? I would like to have a talk with him."

I could hear the whispers of the children echoing through the house, and a fair-haired child peered down at me from a corner on the upper floor.

Upon my mention of Damien, Mrs. Crabtree visibly tensed, taking a step back. "I regret to inform you, Mr. Davison, I am unable to comply with your request. Damien is no longer in our care. I was compelled to send him away after discovering Damien kissing another boy in their quarters last night. Such depravity cannot be tolerated in this household, especially with other children present."

The look of total repulsion must have been evident on my face as she resorted to such retribution over a mere kiss. I felt a surge of anger rising within me. Stepping forward, she began to shrink back.

Addressing Mrs. Crabtree, I stated, "As a devout Christian myself, I find your behavior abhorrent! No child should be entrusted to your care. I was assigned to evaluate your home to determine if it was appropriate for Damian, but after witnessing your mistreatment of a child, sending him out alone into the night to fend for himself, I am compelled to advise against any child being under your supervision! Now, if you would excuse me, I like to see his room. Perhaps I can uncover a clue to his whereabouts."

Mrs. Crabtree moved aside and informed me, "As you wish, Mr. Davison. His room is upstairs to the right."

Upon finding his room, I found the young fair-haired boy I saw earlier seated on his bed. Taking a seat on the adjacent bed, I inquired, "What is your name? Is this where Damien slept?"

The boy was perched at the far end of the bed, with his knees drawn close to his chest.

"I am Brian, and yes, this is Damien's bed. He packed clothes in a backpack and the remaining items; she made me stash them in a corner over there. Please tell Damien I am sorry, I regret lying when she accused him of kissing me. It was actually me who kissed him. I just got scared when she unexpectedly walked in on us. Damien had been exceptionally kind to me since my arrival, and I found him so cute."

I directed my attention to Brian. "You have done nothing wrong. Unfortunately, you must remain cautious, as there are many individuals who struggle to accept those who are different. Her reaction was entirely uncalled for. Hopefully, one day society will accept us for who we are. Once I locate Damien, I will return for his things. First, I must inform my superiors of the situation and then begin searching for a clue to ascertain his whereabouts. Brian, stay strong, and I will do everything in my power to find him."

Brian nodded in appreciation. " Thank you, I do know one place you might look. Damien likes to go down by the river when he wants to think."

Expressing my gratitude to Brian, I headed downstairs, only to find Mrs. Crabtree awaiting me at the entrance. Her face twisted in disdain as she glared at me.

"Demon child," she hissed, "Damien revealed his true nature to me before departing. That boy is evil; he is the offspring of Satan."

Taking a few steps forward, I watched as she recoiled, stumbling against a nearby table as she yelped. "What I find to be evil is individuals such as yourself who pass judgment on others for simply being themselves without considering the harm caused in the process. You claim to be a Christian woman, yet your actions do not align with the true essence of Christianity. Instead, you manipulate the teachings of the Bible to suit your purposes. When you face your creator, it will be your actions that will be judged! Have a pleasant day, Mrs. Crabtree. I will return later to retrieve Damien's belongings."

Exiting the residence, I shut the door behind me. Although I was angry, I made an effort to maintain my composure while effectively conveying my message.

I needed to locate a public payphone to contact Mr. Craft and provide him with an update.

Miss Periwinkle, the receptionist, answered the phone. "Mr. Craft's office, how can I help you?"

I responded, "Good day, Miss Periwinkle, this is Patrick Davison. I need to report to Mr. Craft."

"Certainly, Mr. Davison, please hold for a moment."

After a brief pause, Mr. Craft answered the phone. "Hello, Mr. Davison, how are you progressing?"

I responded, "Not good, I have just returned from the foster house. Mrs. Crabtree kicked Damien out of the house due to an incident of kissing a boy, unjustly placing the blame on him. I am going out to search for him."

Mr. Craft responded, "I had a feeling that this situation might happen. I will consult with the local authorities to gather more information. It is important to note that Damien is a resourceful individual with some street smarts, and this is not his first encounter with such circumstances. He is not defenseless; he possesses a keen understanding of his abilities. Exercise caution, as he may not trust you at first. However, there is a potential avenue to establish trust. I received a police report indicating that a man was apprehended last night for exposing himself in front of a law enforcement officer. Upon being detained, he had no memory regarding the events leading up to his arrest. Additionally, they have a prior record of him attempting to solicit young men."

I responded, "That suggests he may have been compelled. Where did the police indicate the incident took place?"

Mr. Craft chuckled. "You have certainly done your homework. They mentioned he was found by the riverbank. It is not too far from the house."

I felt reassured. "One of the children in the household informed me that Damien tends to frequent the river when he wants to think. At least that provides a starting point for our search. Thank you, Mr. Craft. I will report back later with an update."

Mr. Craft responded, "Best of luck." Armed with that bit of information, I made my way down to the river.

Chapter Eight
Damien

I sprang to my feet, throwing the sheets off me that I'd managed to get myself all tangled in. Glancing around the room, it took me a moment to recognize where I was. I took a few deep breaths. *Okay so last night did happen, and it was not a dream. Now that I was awake, my immediate concerns were two pressing matters on my mind: One, the need to relieve myself, and two, the insistent growling of my hungry stomach.* Fortunately, the first issue was promptly resolved as I spotted a small bathroom at the far end of the room. Stepping inside, I jumped back at the unpleasant odor filling the air as they had neglected to clean the room in some time. I cautiously tested the toilet to see if it was still functioning and was relieved to find that it had running water. After successfully taking care of the first pressing matter, I retrieved a fresh set of clothing from my backpack: A T-shirt paired with red tennis shorts. Since the bathroom was lacking a shower, I improvised by cleaning myself in the sink, utilizing an old T-shirt as a makeshift washcloth. I then hung the damp shirt on the windowsill to dry. Now I needed to address my second pressing matter, my growling stomach.

I proceeded to move the cabinet I had placed in front of the door last night. To my surprise, the cabinet felt much heavier than before. Mental note: I must remember that after my powers wear off, everything becomes a little more challenging. After maneuvering myself between the wall and the cabinet, I used my legs to push it a few feet away from the door, allowing me to exit. Upon stepping outside, I looked around to ensure no one was in sight before heading into town to satisfy my hunger. I found one of my favorite fast food restaurants and entered to place an order. I looked at the menu and made my selection.

A young blonde girl with a ponytail, energetically chewing gum, approached the counter. "May I take your order." She inquired.

I replied, "I would like two hamburgers, a large order of fries, a large soda, a milkshake, and a chocolate chip cookie."

The girl behind the counter let out a giggle. "That will be four dollars and ninety-nine cents." She informed me.

I handed her a twenty-dollar bill, and she returned my change. After waiting a few minutes for my meal, the girl handed me the tray. Finding a seat, I chowed down on the delicious food, a rare treat because we never got stuff like this at home. Despite recognizing that this was just junk food and it probably did not have high nutritional value, nevertheless, being a typical teenager, the taste was too good to resist. I consumed almost everything, deciding to save my cookie for later.

I left the restaurant and headed back towards the river to walk off some of the effects of the meal I had just consumed. The weather was pleasant, and there were people leisurely walking along the riverway. I noticed a young boy, approximately my age, with blondish-red hair sitting on a bench. He was engrossed in sketching something on a pad of paper, but I was too far away to see the details of what it was. Intrigued by what he was working on, I observed him for a while before my curiosity got the best of me. I slowly approached him from behind, pausing for a moment to try to get a clear view of his artwork.

At that moment, the boy spoke, "You know it is considered impolite to stand behind someone while they are drawing."

Apologizing, I responded, "I was just curious about what you were working on."

"Why don't you come around and join me? I will show you. It took you long enough to come over. You have been watching me for a while." The boy suggested with a hint of amusement.

Impressed by his perceptiveness, I remarked, "You were aware that I was watching you? Despite the fact that you have not looked up from your sketchbook for some time."

The boy with the blondish-red hair flashed a grin. "It only took a moment. I have already formulated a mental image of you. You possess jet-black hair almost down to your shoulders, you are of a similar age to me, and you are dressed in a white T-shirt with red shorts and white tennis shoes. Let us not overlook the fact that your eyes are a wonderful shade of blue, or perhaps more purple, and you are extremely handsome."

I just sat there for a brief moment, my mouth slightly open. Then I laughed, "Well, at least you got one thing correct."

The young man with slightly blond hair then looked up from his paper and offered a smile in return.

Seizing the opportunity, I took a closer look at him and noticed something peculiar. "One of your eyes is green. And the other one is blue. Remarkable! That is so cool. I am Damien, by the way, and I do not recall seeing you around here before. May I ask where you are from?"

In response, he introduced himself, "I am Jason, visiting from Dayton, on a field trip from school for my art class. I am drawing the river and bridges in this area. Feel free to look at my work if you like."

Jason opened his sketchbook, showing me some of his drawings.

Impressed, I complimented him, "Your artwork is very good; you have a great eye." As I rested my hand on his shoulder, we both experienced a shock, a sudden surge of his energy passed between us. Inadvertently, I began to absorb some of his life force. Startled, I quickly withdrew.

Jason raised his hands to his forehead. "What happened? I suddenly feel tired."

Thinking quickly, I inquired, "Jason, are you feeling alright? Have you eaten today? Maybe your sugar is low. I have a friend who has diabetes."

He responded, "I had breakfast, but I forgot to eat lunch. I left it on the bus. I was too preoccupied with my drawing."

Turning to him, I offered, " I have this chocolate chip cookie from lunch. Perhaps it will help you feel better." Breaking off a piece, I handed it to him. He accepted it and took a bite.

I reassured Jason, "Let's wait a moment to see if that helps." Afterwards, he took a sip of water.

Grinning, he expressed his gratitude, "Thank you, Damien. Well, that was unusual. I guess I should go back. I left my lunch on the bus."

"Here, have the rest of the cookie. I really should be going too."

Jason's face saddened, "I wish you did not have to leave. I really enjoyed talking with you, but here, take one of my drawings as a memento. Who knows, maybe we will run into each other again one day."

I accepted the drawing graciously and responded with a smile, "I certainly do hope so."

Jason rose from his seat. I watched him walk away. He turned and glanced back, gave a wave before disappearing from view, and then he was gone. Looking around to see if anyone noticed what had happened, but everyone seemed engrossed in their own thing and had not taken notice of what had happened. I began to walk around some more. Then

I stopped and looked at the drawing. I could not help but admire the exceptional talent displayed by the young artist.

I paused at the park and settled onto a bench when I noticed a man that I thought I had seen before, when I was talking to Jason. Okay, *do not jump to conclusions, Damien; it is in the middle of the day. I just got a little juiced up with Jason.* After walking a block and turning onto the next street, I noticed the man was still trailing behind me. I continued for a few more blocks and abruptly picked up the pace. Then I bolted down and around the street until I found myself tailing him. He proceeded for a few more blocks before stopping, looking around, and scratching his head. Just as I was about to sneak up behind him, he spun around.

"Have you had your fun, Damien?" He inquired.

I gave him a curious look. "How do you know my name?"

He laughed. "My name is Patrick Davison, your newly appointed Renfield. So, can we stop playing this cat and mouse game and have a serious conversation?"

A wave of relief washed over me. "I'm glad you are not another one of those perverts trying to pick me up again. Let's go back to the park and talk."

Chapter Nine

Pat

I retrieved the file on Damien from the trunk of my vehicle. It was imperative that I had his photo on hand. Placing the picture in my jacket pocket, I noted that it had been taken a year ago, providing me with a fairly accurate depiction of his appearance. Despite being of a tender age, he is pretty mature for a child of his age, easily passing for a boy quite older than he appears. As I settled into my car, I reviewed the file, setting my expectations for the meeting with Damien, a vampeal, or any supernatural being I had yet to encounter other than spirits.

Upon reaching the river, I got out of my vehicle and strolled to the water's edge, scanning my surroundings in the hopes of locating Damien. I hoped the boy was still around because it was my only lead. Choosing to hold off on asking people about Damien's whereabouts in order to prevent him from running off if he learned that I was searching for him, I initially thought I might walk along the riverway a few times.

Only if my initial search proved pointless did I plan to show the picture to people and ask if they had seen him. The area was teeming with activity that day, with joggers, rollerbladers and walkers dotting the landscape. That is the thing about the late seventies: there is a widespread desire to maintain a slender figure; you can never be too skinny, as represented by the universal presence of supermodels like Twiggy in magazines.

Pausing to gaze at the river, I inhaled the crisp, fresh air. My thoughts drifted to Matt, wondering if he had arrived safely at college. Although it was regrettable that we could not attend at the same time, I took comfort in the fact that he was now able to pursue his education.

Continuing down the river, I observed the passersby until I reached the park. I decided to rest, I unpacked some snacks from a brown paper bag, hoping to blend in with the crowd. Nearby, an elderly lady was feeding the pigeons. Despite her actions, she did not appear to be homeless. Adorned with a neatly pinned hat atop her silver braided hair, she was clean and dressed in a floral print dress and a sweater. She was whistling and engaging in a conversation with the birds, seeming content in her solitude.

Inquiring gently, I asked, "Do you visit the park regularly to feed the birds?"

She replied, "Why, yes. Following the passing of my dear Abner, I cremated him, and I scattered his ashes over the water. I frequently come here to feed the birds when the weather permits."

" I offer my condolences for your loss. How long has it been since your husband passed?" I inquired.

The woman gazed at me intently. "Abner was not my husband. That bastard left me years ago for a younger woman. Abner was my cat and companion."

I accidentally let out a chuckle, "My apologies."

She flashed a smile. "No apology necessary. The tramp took off with all his money and eloped with the gardener."

I almost could not contain my laugh. "Thank you for sharing your story; it truly brightened my day. If you would not mind, could you take a look at this photograph? I am searching for this young boy."

"Is the boy in some sort of trouble?" she inquired.

I responded, "Not at all. I am Patrick Davison from the Department of Social Services. He had a falling out with his foster mother, who kicked him out in the middle of the night. I am endeavoring to relocate him and secure a more suitable living arrangement. The current foster home just was not the right fit for him."

"That sounds dreadful. How could you subject a child to such treatment? I trust you expressed your disapproval to her."

I snickered, "Indeed, I did. I must now evaluate the well-being of the other children in the house."

The elderly woman glanced to my side. "Is that your young man over there?"

I turned and noticed a boy in red shorts walking past us. I figured I would observe him for a moment to avoid any potential embarrassment in case it was not him. He lingered by the river, fixated on something or someone. It was then that I saw what caught his focus. Another young boy, similar in age, with reddish-blond hair, was seated on a bench with a sketchpad. Damien looked like a cat ready to pounce. I wondered if this was his vampire instinct at play. Eventually, he approached the boy from behind, trying to get a closer look at his artwork. Damien remained engrossed for a while before the red-haired kid uttered something without looking up from his drawing pad. The two young men seemed to be having a conversation.

After bidding farewell to the elderly lady, I decided to stroll past them. Damien was too engrossed in the conversation, to take notice of me. As I passed by the two young men, they introduced themselves. I was relieved to have been correct in my assumption. The boy was indeed Damien, while the other boy went by the name of Jason. I chose to observe quietly and refrain from eavesdropping on their conversation. My sole objective was to monitor Damien until the opportune moment presented itself.

I continued walking until I reached a bench about fifty feet away, where I decided to rest. Damien and Jason engaged in a conversation for some time until something peculiar happened, Damien placed his hand on Jason's shoulder, and both of them reacted as though they had received an electric shock. Damien scanned the area to see if anyone had noticed. Prompting me to look away to avoid drawing attention to myself. When I turned back, I observed Damien attempting to console Jason. He retrieved a cookie from his pocket, broke off a sizable piece and offered it to Jason. After Jason consumed the treat, Damien provided him with another piece along with some water. Eventually, Jason rose to his feet, signaling his intention to depart. The two exchanged their farewells.

Recognizing an opportune moment, I decided to approach Damien. I rose from the bench and proceeded towards him, passing Jason along the way. It appeared that Damien noticed me, as he altered his course and began walking in the opposite direction, only to navigate a few blocks before reversing his path. I tried to catch up to him, anticipating his strategy and chose to play along, allowing Damien to close the distance between us. Before long, he reached me, at which point I introduced myself. I informed Damien that I was his new Renfield and had spent the entire day searching for him after learning about the incident at the foster home. Therefore, we agreed to return to the park to engage in a discussion and resolve the matter.

Chapter Ten
Damien

When we returned to the park, I was worried about what was going to happen next. I hoped that I would not be forced to stay at the Crabtree house.

Pat remarked, "It is truly remarkable to witness your capabilities, my friend. You are the first Vampeal that I have encountered."

I responded with a smile, "So they have told you about me?"

As we strolled past the bench where an elderly woman was feeding the pigeons, she looked over at us and smiled. "I see you have found your young man."

Pat graciously replied to her, "Yes, thank you."

I scratched my head and felt like I had missed something. We walked for a while before coming across a bench where we decided to stop and talk.

I informed Pat, "I cannot go back to that house to live. I simply cannot cope with what she believes."

Pat agreed, "You do not have to. You are welcome to spend the night at my place tonight, and together we shall figure out what to do tomorrow. Although we still need to retrieve your things sometime this evening. Furthermore, Brian expressed his regret for deceiving Mrs. Crabtree regarding the incident with the kiss."

I asked him, "So, you also knew about that? It was a shame that it was my first kiss with anyone. You do not find it wrong that I prefer guys?"

Pat hesitated briefly, carefully considering his response. "No, I do not. I am also gay. The city tends to be more tolerant than the smaller towns in Ohio, but you must still be careful. There are a lot of individuals who believe it is wrong, much like Mrs. Crabtree. By the way, it appeared that you were quite taken with the straightaway blond individual in the park earlier."

I laughed softly. "Yes, right up to the moment I zapped him. But, yes, there was something special about him."

Pat inquired, "Is it customary for that to happen when you drain someone's energy?"

I shook my head. "No, that was the first time. It was like there was an additional energy source that triggered a reaction, resulting in a significant jolt. I got scared so I left, and now it is unlikely that I will see him again. Perhaps it is for the best considering what happened."

"You never know, being half vampire, stranger things have happened. Would you care to join me for dinner, and maybe we can order a pizza? You can freshen up, then later we can retrieve your belongings."

Interrupting him, I exclaimed, "Pizza! That is not something we get at the foster home too often. The closest Mrs. Crabtree makes is spaghetti."

We arrived at Pat's house, a two-story country house with a red barn off to the side.

Pat explained, "This is my brother's and my house. It was handed down to us by our late parents a few years ago. They left the family house to both of us. I guess that makes my brother and I orphans as well."

As we entered through the kitchen, I set my backpack on the kitchen table, and we proceeded to the living room.

Pat instructed me, "Please have a seat while I place an order for pizza. What toppings do you like on it?"

I responded, "Pepperoni would be great, thank you."

"One large pepperoni coming right up."

A short time later, Pat entered the living room and took a seat in an old reclining chair. "It should be here approximately thirty minutes."

"Didn't you mention that your brother lives here as well?"

Pat responded, "Indeed, my identical twin brother, although I suspect he will be staying in Florida for an extended period. We were both hired the same day by the Feral Society. He also serves as a

Renfield and is responsible for caring for a sixteen-year-old honor student who is half-dwarven in his third year of college."

Shortly after, we heard the sound of a car pulling up the gravel driveway and honking its horn. "That must be the pizza." Pat rose from his seat, proceeded to the kitchen, and then out the back door. Within a few minutes, he returned carrying a large pizza and a two-liter bottle of soda. "Enjoy it while it is hot."

No need to ask me twice. I folded a slice in half and chowed down. It did not take long for us to finish off the pizza and finish off the soda that he had bought.

Trying to make conversation, I remarked to Pat, "It's remarkable that all this stuff is true. It is said that everyone in the Feral Society has some sort of link to the supernatural. So what about you and your job?"

Pat flashed a grin and replied, "Matt, my sibling has the ability to see the spirits of the deceased, while I possess the gift of hearing them."

My eyes widened in fascination. "That is so cool. You must share some ghost stories with me sometime."

"Of course, there will be plenty of time for that. Well, Damien, it seems you were really quite hungry, as we completely consumed the pizza in no time. Why don't you get yourself cleaned up? The bathroom is located through the door on the right. I will bring you some towels." Pat offered.

"That would be great. So do you mind if I take a long hot shower? We only get a few minutes in the showers at the homes, too many kids."

Pat chuckled and replied. "Certainly, go ahead, it's all yours."
I located the bathroom and closed the door behind me. After I removed my clothes, I stepped into the shower and adjusted the water temperature as hot as I could stand. I stood under the running water, allowing it to wash over my face and body. I then turned to let it run down my back, washing away the accumulated stress of the last few days. In that moment, I could not help but wonder, could things finally be taking a turn for the better? How many more homes would I have to live in? But for now this was great. I heard a knock on the door and Pat poked his head in.

Pat informed me, "Here are the towels, I will put them on the sink."

I responded, "All right, I will be out in a few minutes."

"Take your time, there is no need to rush."

"Thank you, Pat."

I proceeded to lather myself up with soap, followed by shampooing my hair, and finally rinsing myself off. As I pulled back the shower curtain, the room quickly filled with steam. Stepping out of the shower, I reached for one of the towels, drying myself off, and wrapping it around my waist before returning to the living room. There, I found my backpack and pulled out a clean shirt, a pair of shorts, and underwear. It is then I remembered I had left my shirt hanging to dry on the window ledge at the warehouse. Perhaps Pat would permit me to go back and get it. I put my T-shirt on, and I dropped the towel, slid my underwear on and then my shorts.

Pat re-entered the living room and inquired, " How are you feeling?"

"Oh, thank you, it is precisely what the doctor ordered."

"I suppose we ought to proceed to the foster house and pick up the rest of your belongings."

I exhaled. "Very well, let us get this over with."

And thus, Pat and I headed over to Mrs. Crabtree foster home.

Chapter Eleven
Pat

We knocked on the door of the foster home. Mrs. Crabtree greeted us. "Ah, it is you, I see that you located the little demon." She remarked.

I responded, "Indeed, with no assistance from you! We are here solely to retrieve the rest of Damien's belongings."

Mrs. Crabtree's facial expression twisted as she instructed us, "Proceed upstairs to gather your belongings. I trust you will not take too long. Kindly remove your immoral behavior from my house and away from the children."

Disregarding her, we made our way past her and upstairs to the bedroom. We gathered Damien's possessions that were stacked in boxes in the corner. Turning to Damien, I inquired, "Where is Brian?"

Damien looked around. "It is getting late, and he should be in his room."

The little girl with pigtails popped into the room. I bent down to speak to her. "It is a pleasure to see you again. Do you happen to know where Brian is?"

She replied, "Brian was so upset about Damien getting kicked out by Mrs. Crabtree told us that he was going to look for Damien. It is getting dark now, and I am starting to get worried. That was a long time ago. Do you think he is okay?"

placing my hand on her shoulders, I reassured her, "I am confident that he is fine. We will go out and find him. Why don't you return to your room?"

Damien turned to me and inquired, "What are we going to do?"

In response, I expressed, "We will have to go back out and look for him. The authorities will not consider him missing for twenty-four hours. Damien, I have a question. Mrs. Crabtree, other than her Bible obsession, how does she treat the children?"

Puzzled, Damien looked at me and replied. "Well, she makes sure the children are well-fed and clean at all times. She is pretty fair to all the children except for me."

"I believe we must persuade her to abandon her preconceived notions about you being a vampeal. I think you need to compel her. Additionally, maybe tweak her twisted Bible fixation."

Damien pondered for a second, although reluctantly agreed. "I will need to get close to her and extract some of her energy to render her receptive to my suggestions."

We went downstairs to talk with Mrs. Crabtree, in the living room.

I inquired, "Where is Brian? Why is he not in the house?"

She cast a disapproving glance our way. "He told me he was going out, and he would be home later."

"Did he tell you that he was going to look for Damien because he felt guilty for you kicking Damien out last night?"

In response, "Certainly not, I would never condone such behavior. He said that he needed to get some air and went for a run along the river. He should be back at any moment now."

"It is dark already, he should have been home by now."

She inquired, "Should I call the police and report him missing?"

I replied, "You could, however, they typically advise waiting until he has been missing for more than twenty-four hours. Damien and I will have to search for him. You will need to remain patient until then. All of this is your fault, and I do expect to make amends with Damien for your previous action."

I then turned to Damien letting him know my intentions. Damien understood what we needed to do. I was aware that he would prefer any alternative than accept her apology. In the end, it would be in the best interest of the children. Mrs. Crabtree hesitated momentarily. But then she sighed and relented.

"I apologize for my overreaction. Perhaps I should not have insisted that you leave the house last night. I wish you success with your future foster family."

Damien felt the insincerity in her words yet decided to go along with it. "I accept your apology." He stated.

I proposed to Mrs. Crabtree, "Why not offer Damien a hug as a gesture of goodwill?"

Her eyes widened and hesitated briefly, displaying a hint of suspicion, before slowly approaching Damien with open arms. He reciprocated the gesture. Then, he absorbed her energy without raising any suspicions. As she began to feel fatigued and fall limp, we guided her to a chair. Damien looked into her eyes, her pupils dilated, indicating she was ready for my suggestions.

Damien instructed her, "You will not remember seeing my true appearance and fangs; instead, focus on the fact that I am being relocated to a new foster home today. Your primary concern is that Brian has not returned from his run. You will care for your children as a compassionate Christian woman should, without passing judgment based on their race, color, or sexual orientation. Guide them and allow the children to live their lives to the fullest without imposing your beliefs on them. Now, take a moment to rest. When I snap my fingers, you will awaken and remember only what I have told you."

Damien rose and approached me. "It is done." He confirmed

"Excellent, we will wake her shortly, then gather your belongings, place them into the car, and set out to find Brian," I responded.

Damien returned to her side, snapped his fingers, and she regained consciousness.

Confused, she placed her hand on her forehead and asked, "What just happened?"

I explained to her, "You started to feel faint, you must have been working too hard so we assisted you to a chair. How do you feel now?"

"I believe I will be alright, I am just a bit light headed."

I remarked, "Very well, Mrs. Crabtree, we must leave. You ought to rest, and we will attempt to find Brian and bring him back."

She slowly rose from her seat, and we exchanged handshakes. "I wish you success in locating Brian safe and sound and bringing him back home. And Damien, I wish you well with your new foster home."

We expressed our gratitude to her and exited through the front door. Standing on the front porch, I turned to Damien. "I believe that went well."

Damien agreed. Suddenly, he heard a rustling in the trees, prompting us to look upward. Damien saw a figure moving quietly amidst the shadows. Then, a red-haired man perched on the rooftop of the porch. He threw something in Damien's direction, prompting us to rush towards it. As the objects fell to the ground, Damien retrieved them. The red-haired man then swiftly retreated into the shadows of the trees, his laughter echoing as he vanished into the distance. I approached Damien as he displayed the items he had retrieved.

I inquired, "What is it?"

"This is my T-shirt I accidentally left at the warehouse the other night, and the other one belongs to Brian. He was wearing it at the house the night we first met."

"How did they end up here, and who was that lurking in the trees?"

Damien explained, "I encountered a vampire on the night I was kicked out of the house. I suspect the vampire may have come across Brian near the river and taken him to the warehouse."

I remarked, "It appears that is the next destination. Damien, can you recall the location of the warehouse?"

"Certainly, it is just a few blocks away from the park where you found me."

Chapter Twelve
Damien

I explained to Pat the events that happened that night when I had a confrontation with a red-haired vampire. " How he tried to attack me, and in self-defense, I broke his arm. I thought he ran off, but evidently, the vampire must have followed me back to the warehouse. He must have found Brian while searching for me at the river. The Vampire said it was not over, so he must be holding Brian at the warehouse to get back at me. God!, if he harms him, I'm going to rip his head off!"

Pat remarked, "Hopefully, Brian is okay. He wants you to come to the warehouse. You know it's a ploy and probably a trap? So we need to be prepared. Let us go to the trunk of my car and retrieve a book given to me by Mr. Craft yesterday, focusing on mythical creatures. Let us examine the section on vampires."

We retrieved the book from my trunk, and Pat found the chapter on vampires. It mentioned that they are sensitive to sunlight.

I informed Pat, "Regrettably, that information doesn't help us right now; sunrise is still hours away. Furthermore, I have no idea where to find a UV light at this time of night."

We continued reading, discovering two additional methods for eliminating a vampire. One method involves piercing or extracting their heart, although using a wooden stake for this purpose can be risky due to the close proximity required and should only be used if the vampire is incapacitated. Conversely, using a crossbow is a more direct option, provided one is a skilled marksman. The second approach involves decapitating the vampire. While fire and dismemberment may slow them down, it won't kill them, as they have the ability to heal from such injuries over time.

Pat remarked, "It appears that their abilities are on par with yours. Perhaps we can resolve this without resorting to lethal measures, but in the event it comes to that, would you be prepared? I understand this is a lot to ask, especially considering your age; you are only fourteen."

"Why is everyone continuously bringing that up? I am nearly fifteen, and if it comes down to the vampire or myself, I will show him that I do not have little fangs, I can be a formidable opponent."

Pat Snickers, "Did he say you had little Fangs?"

"Please, Pat, do not go there!"

"We should go over to the warehouse and see if we can get Brian back."

We got into the car and paused briefly before proceeding to the warehouse.

Pat inquired, "I'm aware that you recently fed on Mrs. Crabtree's energy, but was it sufficient?"

"I don't know how much I can take. I have never tested my limits. Perhaps a slight boost might be beneficial. I don't want to make you too tired."

Pat confidently stated, "I should be able to handle it. Please, take my hand."

So I did as Pat asked. I grasped his hand for a moment, feeling a surge of energy. Then I let him rest for a moment.

"Pat, how do you feel?"

He reassured me, saying, "I'm fine." Please give me a moment, and I will be back to normal.

"Pat, how does it feel when I do that to someone? It doesn't hurt, does it?"

"No, not at all. I experienced a profound sense of numbness throughout my body, followed by an overwhelming drowsiness, like when you are under sedation when you are in an operating room while counting down from ten. All I desired was to curl up into a fetal position and fall asleep."

"I'm relieved no one suffers when I do it. I realized that I don't need to use my nails unless they resist. I get all juiced up and tingly all over. It's kind of like the ultimate sugar high without the crash."

"We should go. It is uncertain how much longer the vampire will toy with Brian before he hurts him."

I informed Pat of the location. "It's not far from the park. Approximately five or six blocks away in a historic warehouse district."

"Okay, we're off."

We located the warehouse in no time and proceeded downstairs to the storeroom. I effortlessly moved the cabinet aside as Pat illuminated the room with his flashlight, although I found it unnecessary as the lighting was fine. I could see without it. Pat meticulously searched a desk and found several candles, which he proceeded to light using a Zippo lighter that he had in his jacket pocket. Then I caught sight of Brian unconscious on the sofa, where I had slept the previous night. I rushed over to Brian. He was groaning and disoriented but still alive. Upon gently turning his head, I noticed two distinct puncture wounds on his neck, from which a little trickle of blood was dripping. A surge of anger coursed through me. Suddenly, I heard someone clapping from the corner of the room. Pat directed the beam of the flashlight towards the source of the sound, revealing the red-haired vampire from the shadows.

He remarked, "Poor Damien, do you have affection for this human? That is truly heart-wrenching. We had a brief conversation while we were waiting for you to arrive. What a chatty young man. He recounted the entire story of the last few days. But did he not betray you, Damien?

You should be cautious in placing your trust in others. He would kill you the same as he would kill me if you knew what you were."

I could sense the intense surge of rage building up inside me, as it started to consume my entire being. "Brian better be okay or I swear, I will rip you apart."

"I hope your actions will match the severity of your threats. Rest assured, he will survive, for the time being. I am considering making him my pet once I have settled our score for what you did last night. Do you comprehend how much it hurts to mend a broken arm? I had to consume numerous young lives from the streets to get my strength back. I doubt anyone will miss a handful of homeless street rats. However, despite all of that, I am still curious what your blood tastes like, you half-breed."

I turned to the red-haired vampire and said, "I'm giving you one last chance. Get out of here and leave us all alone, or I promise you won't be able to carry out that threat. I will make sure this will be the last night you will ever see."

Pat came over to join us. Then the vampire remarked, "I am contemplating whether I should eliminate your loyal Renfield before your very eyes, my dear vampeal."

Pat responded, "You can try, give it a shot."

The vampire suddenly lunged towards Pat. I really didn't have time to think. I just reacted on instinct, and my lightning reflexes kicked in, and in a blink of an eye, my claws viciously tore into the vampire's face. Blood splattered all over the white sheets. The vampire grabbed his face, but not before I could see that I had ripped his skin and exposed the bone underneath, as bile filled the back of my throat. Then he directed his gaze towards me and uttered a menacing hiss in anger. That gave Pat a second to react. He reached down and forcefully broke off a leg from an end table and embedded it deeply into the vampire's back. The vampire let out a piercing scream of agony as he sharply twisted his head back in the direction of Pat.

The vampire uttered, "Fool, you missed the heart. I'm going to enjoy killing you both for what you have done to me."

I shouted at the vamp, "I told you. You will never get the chance!"

I embedded my claws deep into his chest, ripping out his heart. Then I held it for a second and crushed it. The vampire turned back to me. I could see the anguish in his eyes. His body started to rot and decay, then finally burst into flames, and ash floated through the air.

I let out a weary sigh. "Pat, why did he make me do that?"

Pat responded, "It is uncertain; we may never know the answer. Sometimes certain individuals simply are just self-destructive."

I heard Brian start to come around. I went over to him. "Are you alright?"

"Damien, is that you? Some guy brought me here and attacked me. He told me you were staying here. I'm sorry. I got you into trouble with Mrs. Crabtree."

" Don't worry, Brian. The red-haired guy is gone. You're safe now, and it all worked out. I'm fine."

Pat informed us, "We should leave. Brian can spend the night at my house tonight. I will take him back to the foster home tomorrow morning. I need to call Mrs. Crabtree when we get home to let her know you are alright."

We returned to Pat's house, and we got cleaned up. Brian and I sat on the couch in each other's arms. I gave him a kiss, and I put my head on his chest and started to fall asleep. Afterwards, I sensed Pat gently draping a blanket over both of us. Later on, we drifted off to sleep as we nestled in each other's arms.

Chapter Thirteen

Pat

The following day, we returned Brian to the foster home. Both Brian and Damien seemed hesitant to get out of the car, but I reassured them that it would be alright. I proceeded to knock on the door, and to my surprise, Mrs. Crabtree greeted us. Her demeanor was unexpectedly pleasant. As she displayed a genuine smile and appeared noticeably at ease, strands of her hair flowed down elegantly, framing her face nicely.

She pleasantly greeted us, "Hello," in a gentler tone other than her usual voice. "I'm so relieved that you found Brian so quickly and that he was unharmed."

I turned to Brian and Damien and instructed them, "Say your goodbyes, boys, for we have a busy agenda ahead of us today."

Damien grasped Brian's arm and drew him in close. To Brian's astonishment, Damien pressed a lingering kiss upon his lips. I averted my gaze as they intertwined in an embrace.

Mrs. Crabtree exclaimed, "Oh, how delightful, Brian. Please come inside, my young man, and allow Damien and Mr. Davison continued on their way."

Brian was stunned, and he turned to me puzzled, "Okay, what got into her."

Damien and I exchanged glances, our smiles mirroring each other."We sat her down and had a little discussion, managing to sway her towards a more enlightened perspective." I remarked.

Brian simply smiled, shook his head, and proceeded to enter the house.

Damien inquired, "Where are we off to now?"

"Damien, have you ever visited the office?"

He beamed with enthusiasm and exclaimed, "That is really cool."

Damien and I proceeded to the Feral Building and made our way to Miss Periwinkle's office.

She inquired, "Greering, Mr. Davidson, is this young man Damien?"

"Yes, indeed. We have come to see Mr. Craft, would you please notify him that we are here?"

"Certainly, Mr. Davidson, I shall see if he is currently available." With that, she knocked on the door and entered Mr. Craft's office.

Damien seized my arm and informed me, "I'm not very comfortable in an office like this. Typically, most stuffed shirts are usually shipping me off to some foster home."

I reassured him, " It will be alright, Mr. Craft may appear to be a cantankerous old bulldog, but he is surprisingly nice."

Miss Periwinkle emerged from the office and made her way towards us. "Mr. Craft is ready to see you now. You may proceed to the rear offices located behind the bookcase. Do you recall which book you need to pull?"

I replied. "Yes, indeed, I do appreciate it, Miss Periwinkle."

Damien and I entered Mr. Craft's office, I grasped the collection of Edgar Allan Poe's works, causing the bookcase to slide open. As Damien stood there motionless, I glanced over to see his astonishment, his jaw dropping in awe.

I laughed and gently pressed my finger against his jaw to prompt him, "Come on, let's go, Damien."

He trailed behind me as I made my way into the hallway. Upon locating Mr. Craft's office. I proceeded to politely knock on the door.

"Please come in, Mr. Davison."

I swung open the door, and we stepped into the office.

Mr. Craft graciously gestured towards the chairs, " Please, take a seat, gentlemen. I would like to extend my congratulations to you, Mr. Davison, congratulations on your successful completion of your first assignment. You discovered Damien and Brian unharmed and in good health. I am pleased to have the opportunity to finally meet you, Mr... What do I call you? Oh yes, Mr. Lampir. If I recall, that translates to vampire in Bosnian, quite clever, young man. I regret that you were placed in a foster home with a person of such strong religious convictions. We will need to investigate the household to ensure the well-being of the other children."

"I believe the children will be fine. Damien and I engaged her in a conversation, gently persuading her to refrain from being overly judgmental towards her children."

Mr. Craft remarked, "Oh, I presumed you compelled her."

I chuckled, "Indeed, it seems that her behavior has undergone a profound change when she is around Damien and the other children now. Additionally, Damien and I found ourselves in a confrontation with a vampire. It harbored a deep-seated resentment towards Damien. He also retaliated by taking one of the other children from the home and admitted to preying on some vulnerable homeless teenagers; therefore, we may need to investigate the matter further. We attempted to persuade him to leave; however, he proceeded to attack us, forcing us to kill him in self-defense."

Mr. Craft arched an eyebrow and flashed a grin, "Indeed, you are correct. We shall investigate the disappearance of the teenagers. I regret that you felt compelled to use deadly force, but Damien, that is a truly remarkable feat for someone your age."

"Thank you, Mr. Craft, however, I didn't do it alone; it was also due to the expertise possessed by Pat."

" I concur, and I believe the two of you make a great team. The next step is to secure a new and proper foster residence for Damien."

I inquired of Mr. Craft, "If I may be so bold… I have been contemplating the idea of welcoming a foster child into my home in the future. Therefore, if you would be so kind, I would like to extend an invitation to Damien to reside with me."

Mr. Craft applauded. "I was eagerly anticipating that question. I believe that would be a splendid arrangement. Damien, what are your thoughts?"

I glanced over at Damien and observed his gaping mouth opening once more. I leaned forward and gently closed it. Then Damien sprang into action and threw his arms around me in a warm embrace.

Damien exclaimed, "Are you truly proposing that I live with you and your brother permanently? No more shifting from home to home, then Yes, I would love to accept your offer!"

Mr. Craft stated, "Excellent, I shall draft the documents and contact you for your signature once they are prepared."

I expressed my gratitude to Mr. Craft inquired if that would be all, as both Damien and I were in need of some rest."

"By all means, go home and get some rest, as both of you rightfully earned it."

Damien and I exchanged pleasantries with Mr. Crafts before exiting his office. We bid farewell to Miss Periwinkle as we made our way out of the building. Just then, I caught sight of a familiar face as she entered the premises. It was the woman who fed the pigeons, whom I had encountered at the park.

She smiled and inquired, "I trust that everything has worked out for you and Damien?"

"Yes, I believe so, and I am grateful for your assistance. If you would be so kind as to indulge my curiosity, may I ask who you might be?"

She replied, "I am no one really important. You may refer to me as Tellus, although I have been known by many names throughout my eternal existence. Please consider me a friend. Our paths will cross again, and we will continue our conversations."

In response, " Farewell, Tellus. Have a pleasant day."

She graciously smiled as she entered the building, while we headed to the car.

Damien inquired, "Who was that lady? I have seen her before"

"I am uncertain, but I believe that we will see her again."

Damien flashed a mischievous grin and asked, "Since I will be living in your house, may I date Brian and invite him to come over?"

"Damien, you are only fourteen years of age."

"Nearly fifteen within a month or so."

I smiled and informed Damien, "You are hiding a significant secret from Brian, and it remains uncertain whether he will be able to accept you being a Vampeal. Furthermore, it is imperative to exercise caution when disclosing to anyone that you are gay. There are numerous individuals who share similar sentiments to those expressed by Mrs. Crabtree towards us. You cannot simply go around compelling everyone who harbors animosity towards the gay community."

Damien attempted to manipulate me with a sorrowful expression. Then he stated, "I will tell Brian at the opportune moment, and we shall exercise caution in revealing our sexual orientation to others. I give you my word."

I simply shook my head and said, "We shall see, you mischievous little devil."

The End.

Shattered Recollection

Damien the Devil
Book 2

Chapter One
Damien

I am constantly thinking about the events that happened that night and comparing them to what we told everyone about what went on that evening.

Pat and I rescued Brian from an angry vampire who had a grudge against me in the basement of the abandoned warehouse. The authorities, in collaboration with the Feral Society, successfully prevented the events at the warehouse from being disclosed in the mainstream media to protect the three of us from the public eye and to ensure that a story about a vampire did not spread.

In the process, they had to relocate the deceased homeless children discovered in the rear of the warehouse to a different location. They altered the story, centering it around a homeless man living on the streets while under the influence of PCP, also known as angel dust. It was reported that he attacked and robbed some of the homeless children before killing them and leaving them to die, disposing of the bodies under one of the bridges.

If you are curious about what the Feral Society is, in part, it is an organization dedicated to supporting supernaturally gifted children and helping them fit into society. Additionally, after the children come of age, the Feral Society intervenes when the conventional authorities are unable to handle certain situations.

Brian and I are in a wonderful place in our relationship. We have been seeing each other ever since that day—yet I still have not found the courage to tell him that I am a vampeal or to reveal the truth surrounding the tragic death of the homeless kids. I am hesitant to bring up the subject right at the moment because Brian's recollection of that night is somewhat hazy. Occasionally, he looks at me strangely, as if he is trying to remember something and just can't.

I recently celebrated my fifteenth birthday over the summer, while Brian just turned seventeen and now stands a full six inches taller than me. Despite his height, he still remains slender with shaggy blond hair. Brian acquired his driver's license and received some money from his trust fund on his birthday, which he used to buy a slightly pre-owned car. In addition to his new responsibilities, he helps out running errands for Mrs. Crabtree from time to time. Being the eldest child in the house, Mrs. Crabtree granted Brian permission to move into the attic to provide him with his own personal space. She also allows me to come over anytime I want to see him as long as we both keep up our grades.

Pat and Mrs. Crabtree continues to enforce the rule about staying out too late on school nights, and they request that I use the front door.

That doesn't mean I don't try to sneak in now and then when they are not looking. It is a lot more convenient now that I figured out that I can leap to the second story of the house with ease. Brian still thinks I climb up and down the trellis. At times, it scares me that Brian is growing up faster than I am and will probably go off to college soon, leaving me behind.

After settling into Pat and Matt's house, I began putting away the few things I owned. When I looked in my backpack, I found something I'd forgotten about: a drawing that came from a boy I met at the park the next day after I got kicked out of the Crabtree house. That part of the day is somewhat fuzzy in my memory due to the events that happened that night. What was his name? I cannot quite recall…Ah, Jason, that was it. I believe he was a young man with blondish red hair, about my age. He was seated on a bench in the park, engrossed in sketching the bridges that spanned the river. I took a seat beside him to observe his work. A peculiar thing happened when I touched him, causing both of us to experience a sudden jolt, inadvertently transferring some of his energy. While I was okay, Jason appeared momentarily disoriented. In an attempt to assist him, I offered him a portion of my cookie that I had saved from lunch to see if it would help, which he seemed fine after a few minutes. Afterward, he went back to his school bus to get the lunch he had forgotten. Overwhelmed by fear, I panicked and hastily ran off. Later that day, I encountered Pat for the first time before everything happened that night. I think I will give the drawing to Pat for safekeeping for now. I wonder whatever happened to the young boy.

Pat is currently away on a trip, while Matt has returned from Florida to look after me. He is primarily a cool, laid-back uncle and happens to be Pat's identical twin brother. They have the same short brown hair; however, Pat wears glasses and Matt does not, and Matt tends to be more lenient with me compared to Pat. It is not Matt's fault, as Pat tends to take the parenting thing very seriously sometimes. I may protest occasionally, but I am very fond of them both. They are the only family I've ever known, and I'm not sure what it's like to have a traditional family anyway. Nonetheless, I am trying to figure it all out. I guess it is the same among kids my age. We are all doing our best to make sense of the hand life has dealt us.

It's nice having my own bedroom on the second floor with Matt's room right across from me, not that he is here that often to use it. Pat's room is downstairs next to the study, and I am glad that there are two bathrooms, one upstairs and one downstairs. One of my favorite things in the house is the fireplace in the living room that I like to sit in front of for hours, watching the flames dance back and forth. We have a barn next to the house, but never use it—well, except when Brian and I fool around in there sometimes, but that's a story for later.

Mr. Craft told us that after they discovered the bodies of the homeless teenagers, it might have been a newly turned vampire, a fledgling abandoned by its sire left unattended to go on a rampage, and that I inadvertently got caught up in the ordeal that night. Despite the vampire being a real jerk, I am still dealing with the consequences of his death. I am required to attend therapy sessions once a week to process the events of that night and what I did. When I looked into his eyes, I could see real sorrow behind them before he turned to dust. I'm still shocked that they really do that. Then I glanced over at Brian lying there on the sofa, praying that he wasn't hurt.

I am so relieved that Brian has no recollection of that particular night. Who knows what he went through? One thing I'm certain of is that I could never tell him what happened to those teenagers. I pray he never finds out; I am uncertain of how he would react if he found out. In fact, I am unsure what I would have done if I saw the vampire feeding upon someone. Although vampeals do not possess a bloodthirsty nature, I sometimes wonder if our consumption of too much life energy could potentially become addictive over time. The Society provides individuals whom I can feed on if necessary, thus preventing accidentally draining someone by mistake again like I did when I was younger at one of the previous foster homes. If I ever did that to Brian, I would never be able to forgive myself.

I don't know how I'm ever going to get some sleep. I keep wondering what he is doing and if he is thinking about me as well. At least I will see him tomorrow when he comes over.

Chapter Two
Brian

I can hear someone's voice, though I could not quite make it out. *Damien, is that you?* I attempted to open my eyes, yet the strain was too hard. Why am I unable to concentrate? What is wrong with me? I managed to open my eyes slightly, only to find everything a bit hazy. I can barely make out two figures engaged in a conversation, neither of whom appears to be Damien. I strain to hear what they are saying, but I just can't. I wanted to move and shake myself out of this, yet I just lie there motionless, unable to move a finger.

I try to remember what I was doing before I found myself in this situation. Yes, I think I recall—I went out looking for Damien after he was kicked out of the house by Miss Crabtree. God, it was all my fault. I should never have been tempted to kiss him, but I wanted to so badly ever since I arrived at the house. Afterwards I ran into some red-haired guy who informed me that he met Damien and let him crash here for the night.

But where is this place, and where am I? It is extremely hard to concentrate; my head is splitting. *Think, Brian, think.* I was down by the river when I ran into this guy. He said Damien and several other kids were staying at some abandoned warehouse. Reluctant as I was, I felt I had to go with him. We proceeded to the side of the building, where a set of stairs led down to a basement storeroom illuminated by a few candles. Inside, there were numerous sheets thrown over some furniture, and it was at that moment I spotted Damien's t-shirt resting on the sofa. I called out his name, and suddenly, everything went dark—until this very moment. Now I can start to make out what they are saying: two individuals engaged in a heated discussion, seemingly unconcerned if I overheard them or not. One of them was the young man responsible for bringing me here, yet the other remained concealed beneath a hooded robe, hiding its face from view. Whoever it was warned the red-haired guy, "You are meddling in affairs that do not concern you and will meet the same fate as your deceased mentor. You must leave Damien alone. It took a long time to locate where they had hidden him all these years. It is likely they are probably going to move him again. Get rid of this boy and fix this matter tonight, or there will be consequences."

The red-haired guy grinned smugly, still standing his ground. "What are you going to do, kill me?"

"There are far worse things we could do than ending your life. You were supposed to observe Damien, not interfere with him."

"What is so special about this halfling and this boy whom he admires?"

"Damien is none of your concern, but this boy… There is something unusual about him. He is not what he seems. Now look, I believe that your bait is starting to come around."

At that moment, they turned and shifted their gaze towards me, causing me to gasp for air.

I awoke from a vivid dream, catching my breath. Startled, I sat straight up in my bed, looking around the room, momentarily disoriented. Beads of sweat ran down my forehead and chest. Oh dear! That must have been one hell of a dream, and it appears that I have been having a lot of them lately. I attempted to recall what it was about but I couldn't. I only succeeded in giving myself a headache. I pushed the covers aside and perched on the edge of the bed. Suddenly, I turned my head sharply as I heard the sound of someone tapping at my bedroom window.

I felt a sense of relief upon realizing that it was just Damien. Although he did look somewhat like a terrifying villain creeping around in a horror movie, with his striking black hair and his captivating lavender eyes, I was truly happy to see him. Hastily, I made my way over to the window and discreetly let him in before anyone could hear him from downstairs.

"Damien, what are you doing? You know you're not supposed to be here this late. Mrs. Crabtree and Pat will be terribly upset with us if they discover you here."

"Pat is currently away, while Matt is staying with me. I couldn't sleep, so I quietly snuck out and had to see you for a few minutes. I was hoping to get a kiss before bed."

"Alright but just for a moment. You have to be very quiet so we do not disturb Mrs. Crabtree."

I embraced Damien to give him a hug and a tender kiss. A shiver ran down my spine as a gust of cool air from the open window hit my bare skin.

As Damien started to put his arms around me, he pulled back slightly. "Brian, why are you all sweaty?"

"Oh, it's nothing, I just woke up from a strange dream."

"Do you remember what the dream was about, and would you like to talk about it?"

"I would love to; however, I cannot really remember what it was about."

"Have you experienced a lot of strange dreams lately?"

"Yes, they began about a week ago, and I have had a difficult time sleeping. Nevertheless, I am okay. I guess you do not want to touch me now that I'm hot and sticky."

"Oh, do not be ridiculous. I like you in any way that I can get you. However, if you keep having these dreams, please let me know. If you can recall any details, we can try to figure out why you are having them."

"Very well, my sweet. I will try to remember. Perhaps I will put a notebook on the nightstand and write down anything that I can recall, if that makes you happy."

"Excellent, we can review them later. Maybe we should get one of those books on dreams if they have any at the library at school."

"That sounds cool, but let's shift our focus from dreams—wasn't there a reason you came here tonight?"

"Oh yeah, how could I possibly forget about my kiss? Then I better get home before they catch us again."

"I was thinking the same thing. Now come here, you little devil."

Chapter Three
Damien

I sneaked back into the house as quickly and silently as I could, only to discover a figure sitting on the sofa in the dimly lit living room. Crap! It was Matt with his arms folded, looking just as stern as his identical twin brother Pat. With the flick of a switch, I just stood in the doorway frozen, fully aware I was busted.

"Damien, for a vampeal your stealth skills leave something to be desired. However, you are up against the master of sneaking out."

"I'm sorry Matt, I just couldn't sleep and I know I shouldn't be out this late but I just had to see Brian one last time before I went to bed. Are you upset with me?"

"No, not particularly, as long as you do not get caught and get me in trouble with my brother. Because if you do, I will deny any involvement. I remember the passion of young love and how hard it is to pry yourself away from someone you love. However, you know that Pat would not approve, particularly after what happened with the past encounter with the vampire. We're still trying to find out why a fledgling was left to his own devices."

"I know, which is precisely the reason why I need to keep a close eye on Brian. It was my fault that he found himself in that situation."

"Damien, the events of that night were not the responsibility of anyone except the vampires."

"I guess you're right, but when I went over to his house Brian told me that he has been having bad dreams and waking up drenched in sweat. Yet, he is unable to remember what they are about when he wakes up. I am starting to wonder how much he will recall about that night, and the dreadful experiences he went through."

"I know you probably wish Pat was here to discuss this matter, nevertheless, I think you just need to give it some time and let it come out naturally."

"But Matt, what if he discovers that I am a vampeal and freaks out? I'm afraid of losing him."

"Well, speaking from the perspective of a person who struggles with letting anyone in, that is the risk we all face when we open our hearts to someone. You should not copy my past mistakes, I messed up quite a few chances to be happy. By the way, while you are standing there, would you kindly fetch us some drinks and join me on the sofa beside your Uncle Matt?"

I suppressed a chuckle and made my way to the refrigerator, grabbing a beer for Matt and a soda for myself. I noticed a bag of chips on the counter, so I swiftly snatched them up, passed Matt his beer, and settled on the edge of the couch, crossing my legs.

"Matt, have you ever had a boyfriend?"

"No one has really lasted that long, typically a month or two. Damien, I know it has been challenging for you over the years. You are starting a romantic relationship with a great guy, and the future of any relationship is uncertain. However, at least you have the opportunity to find out where it can lead. Pat never dated anyone until he met Steven in college. And for me, I started earlier than my brother, but mostly I had sex on the road or at some out of the-way bar. I have never taken the time to commit to anyone for any real length of time. You got a head start on both of us. I overheard your conversation with Brian regarding his potential enrollment in college within the next year or so. You may stay together, you may not, so I suggest enjoying the moments you two have now."

"I know, I find it hard to plan that far ahead. Nevertheless, it does make me a little sad when I think about it."

"That's life, kiddo. We have to take the good with the bad. The experiences when we are young shape who we are later in life, and there will be numerous individuals who will accept who you are. For those who do not, then fuck 'em, they're not worth it. Sorry, I know my brother is probably better at giving advice than I am."

I grinned. "I believe the college environment is starting to rub off on you a little. It's just nice to have someone to talk to for a change. I doubt Pat would have been as understanding as you were tonight about my sneaking out of the house. Although I know he cares, he tends to be a little uptight sometimes."

"Yep, he has always been that way. However, I believe it is time for bed, young man. What sort of uncle would I be if I let you stay up all night? Now go up to bed and stay there, please. We will see if we can find out more about Brian's dreams later. And do stop worrying so much; you will turn into an old vampeal before your time."

I just laughed as I put away the chips and disposed of the soda can before heading upstairs to my bedroom. I slipped out of my jeans and shirt, throwing them on the chair, and pulled on a nightshirt and shorts. As I nestled under the blanket, my thoughts drifted back to Brian and our kiss, then eventually I quietly fell asleep.

Chapter Four
Brian

Waking up to the annoying sound of an alarm clock is truly a pain. In my attempt to silence it, I accidentally caused it to fall off the nightstand in the process. I let out a sigh and just lay there as I didn't get a lot of sleep last night.

I awoke drenched in a cold sweat again, yet this time I managed to remember a little more of my dream—still only brief images flashed through my mind of the dimly lit warehouse, Damien's t-shirt on the sofa, and a conversation between the red-haired guy and a cloaked figure. However I cannot remember more than that. Why can't I remember? In frustration, my head started to throb like the beat of a drum.

I needed to quickly write down my thoughts before I forget them so that I can go over them with Damien later. Then, I better go down to the kitchen and assist in preparing breakfast for the rest of the kids before Mrs. Crabtree comes pounding on my door. All the children in the foster home have their assigned chores, and that is my designated duty.

I sincerely wish Damien was still here. I remember when I first arrived, he made the mundane task of washing dishes seem more enjoyable. However, he is better off staying with Pat and Matt than living in yet another foster home, as the relationship between Damien and Mrs. Crabtree failed to get along. Nevertheless, over time she turned into a kind-hearted lady and is now fond of Damien. I am pleased that he found a stable and nurturing place to call home, even though I will eventually have to leave.

After splashing my face with water, attending to my morning routine, and dressing myself, I head downstairs to the kitchen where Mrs. Crabtree has already started whipping up breakfast.

She turns to me, gives me a gentle smile before tilting her head, looking concerned. "Brian, are you feeling alright? You appear slightly flushed this morning."

"I'm fine, Mrs. Crabtree, I haven't been sleeping too well lately. I've just been having some bad dreams, but I promise I'll be fine."

Not entirely convinced, she comes over and gently places her hand on my forehead. "It appears that you are not running a fever. If you like, I can take you to see the doctor and he can look you over?"

"No, please don't do that. I assure you, I will be fine. I have been looking forward to seeing Damien and spending the whole day together.

It is Labor Day weekend so we get an extra day off from school this week."

Mrs. Crabtree raised her eyebrow. "Very well, Nevertheless, if this issue continues much longer, I may need to insist the doctor come and look you over thoroughly. The last thing I need is all the children in the house coming down sick with something."

I nodded. "Understood, Damien and Pat would be right behind you if they thought something was wrong."

At that moment, the rest of the children in the house began pouring in and taking their positions to prepare the table for breakfast. The morning conversation around the table was typical as everyone enjoyed their breakfast. Afterwards, we all cleaned up the kitchen and started lining up for the two bathrooms in the house: the boys' facilities upstairs and the girls' situated downstairs.

The oldest of us assisted the younger children with their baths before we took our showers, but I opted to postpone mine and have it over at Damien's place where hot water was more likely to be available. Despite there being two water heaters in the basement of the foster house, there was still never enough hot water to go around.

I gathered my belongings and stuffed them into my backpack, said goodbye to Mrs. Crabtree and the rest of the kids, and then I was out the door. I got into my sporty white 1975 Mustang convertible and drove over to Damien's house.

Chapter Five
Damien

I was just finishing up the breakfast dishes when I heard Brian pull up to the house. After drying my hands, a knock echoed at the back door, and I caught sight of Brian grinning at me through the kitchen window.

I smiled warmly, tossing the dish towel aside, rushing over to greet him. "Ah, there you are, I've been waiting for you all morning."

"Damien, you are well aware that it takes time to get the kids ready for the day, or have you perhaps forgotten since you live in this big old country house?"

I playfully brushed Brian aside and gave him a pouty look. "Brat, you depict me as a modern-day Little Orphan Annie under the care of Daddy Warbucks. Frankly, I am a little scared that in a few years I will age out of the system and have to move on, facing the prospect that I will be on my own again."

"I don't think Pat and Matt are going to make you move out until you're ready to find your own place. I think they care about you too much. Do not forget I'm going to age out myself next year, but at least

I already made arrangements to attend college. Perhaps you should consider exploring that option, or as an alternative, consider starting a work career."

"I am aware of the situation. I wish I were more like you, planning your whole life out already. As for me, I have no idea, and it makes me sad to think about it. Just when I found someone I can relate to, you have to leave. It's been that way my whole life."

"My sweet Damien, I understand how you feel, but it happens to a lot of people. Just because we will not be together does not mean we won't care for each other. Besides, I will not be leaving until next year. We still have plenty of time to spend together, if you still want to. But let's not talk about that now. Yet, we have more pressing matters to discuss. This morning, I had another dream in which I was able to remember a little more about it. It revolved around the night you left the house, and I got attacked by that weird red-haired guy."

At times, I hate being right. Brian is starting to remember what happened that night. "So how much do you remember?"

"Before we dig into the topic at hand, may I use your shower again? You know how quickly we run out of hot water at the house, and I'm starting to get a little smelly."

I smiled, inhaling deeply and playfully covering my nose before bursting out laughing. "I am kidding, you're perfectly fine. Are you really going to leave me hanging while you shower?"

Brian simply smiled and nodded his head, pressing his lips against mine as I gave him a warm embrace.

" Brian, I am starting to suspect the only reason you like me is because I have my own private bathroom."

"Don't be silly, Damien, that is not the only reason. We can talk more about the dream after I take a shower. I do not care what you say; I really need one."

Again, I teased him and flashed a sly smirk. "Yep, I was wondering where that smell was coming from."

He laughed and planted a final kiss on my cheek before disappearing behind the bathroom door. Taking a seat on the couch, I greeted Matt as he came down the stairs and entered the living room.

"Has Brian confiscated our shower again?"

"Yeah, he just got in."

"Alright, I have some running around to do today, probably be back in a few hours. Please try to stay out of trouble while I am away. There is plenty of food in the house, so feel free to fix yourselves something for lunch. Will see what we can do for dinner this evening."

"Very well, see you when you get back. By the way, Brian had another dream this morning and was able to recall more details this time."

"That is very interesting. I am starting to think the vampire compelled him that night, and he started to resist it. It is very rare for a human to break a vampire's compulsion. Do you think there's something special about Brian?"

"I don't think so. I cannot sense anything out of the ordinary about him."

"He must have a remarkably strong will. We will have to look into this matter, but don't push it. Allow it to unfold naturally. He might get headaches or migraines, and who knows what kind of damage he might suffer if he pushes himself too hard. Nevertheless, we can talk about this later. I will need to do some research on the subject and determine the proper way to go about it."

"Very well, Matt. I won't push it. I will let him set the pace."

"I better get out of here so you both can enjoy yourselves, but not too much fun—don't want to see anyone getting pregnant." Matt chuckles as he exits through the kitchen door. Though I chuckled as well, yet, it got me thinking. Brian and I have not really brought up the topic of sex; I know it's going to come up sometime. I have not gone that far with anyone yet. While we have made out and kissed a lot, and I do get aroused when he touches me, I am uncertain if I am ready for more. He is seventeen and nearly a year older than me, and I wonder whether he is still a virgin. Based on what Matt told me, it sounds like Pat and he waited until they were older. The mere thought of it makes me feel a little uneasy.

I was startled when Brian burst out of the bathroom with a towel draped around his waist, water dripping down his chest and forming droplets that fell onto the wooden floor. As he walked around the room, I laughed upon noticing that he had an additional towel wrapped around his head. Brian went over to his backpack and pulled out a blue pair of underwear and black shorts, and he slid the underwear under the towel and over his backside, letting the towel fall to the floor. Brian turned to face me and stood there with his hands on his hips. I was left speechless by the sight before me, prompting me to turn away.

Brian simply smiled. "What, you are not embarrassed to see me in my underwear, are you?"

I had to clear my throat, hoping my voice did not crack and trying to maintain my composure not to sound like a silly little boy. "Of course not, well, perhaps just a little."

Brian picked up his shorts, approached me, put his arms around my waist, and gave me a gentle kiss on my lips. Overwhelmed by his affection, I found myself melting in his arms. Though we had yet to determine our plans for today, for now, I just wanted to make this moment last as long as possible.

Chapter six
Brian

It felt comforting to be in Damien's arms without having to worry about what everyone was going to think. However, it dawned on me that I was standing there only in my underwear and I was beginning to get aroused. Feeling a little embarrassed, I gently slipped out of his arms and quickly put on my shorts. Damien grabbed my arm and gave me a disappointed look.

"Brian is everything alright?"

I gave him a sheepish grin, praying that Damien did not notice that my face felt really warm. "I am just fine, Damien. I simply needed to put on my shorts before you… how can I put this… saw a little more of me than I think we are both prepared for."

Damien did not turn away; instead, he just returned the grin and casually reached down and adjusted his package in his own jeans.

"Brian, I know we have not yet had the opportunity to discuss the topic of sex. There's something that you should know. As you may have figured out, I have never done anything with a boy other than my limited experience kissing you."

"It is perfectly all right, I do not have a lot of experience myself. Despite the fact that I am older than you, I would never push you into doing something that you are not ready for. However, I trust that will not stop us from making out every chance we get. When the time is right, we will know."

Damien laughed mischievously, pushing me onto the sofa and firmly pinning me down. It made me think that he is exceptionally strong, and it would be truly difficult for anyone to force him to do anything against his will.

"Alright, I surrender. What would you like to do today, my dear? Shall we visit the park or perhaps catch a movie or something?"

Damien just looked at me and contemplated for a moment before responding, "I realize this might sound silly, but if you are willing, I would like to do something that I never really got the chance to do at the foster homes."

I looked at Damien with a little hesitation on my face. "And what would that be?"

"Well, we have all this food in the house. Wouldn't it be a splendid idea to pack a bunch of stuff and have a picnic?"

"Wow, you have never experienced a picnic before? I believe that is a splendid suggestion. Where would you prefer to have it?"

"What about the old barn situated behind the house? You know how I like fooling around in there with you… There's a loft with numerous bales of hay, and we can open the doors and air the place out."

"Damien, are you propositioning me for a roll in the hay?"

Damien snickered softly. "Perhaps just a little. However, it is a nice place where we can talk and be ourselves. Pat and Matt seldom go out there anymore."

"You know I have not been on a picnic for quite some time myself, not since my parents passed away. I think it would be a great spot to designate as our special place when I come over."

"Very well, the matter is settled then. Shall we grab some blankets and prepare a feast fit for a king."

We swiftly jumped from the sofa and began our preparation. Damien retrieved some blankets from the closet for us to lay on, while we made ham sandwiches on white bread with Swiss cheese and mustard. I located a Tupperware container and filled it with an assortment of grapes and berries, as Damien grabbed some soda and chips. Lacking a proper picnic basket, we improvised and recycled a cardboard box. Afterward, we made our way to the barn and the old wooden ladder leading to the loft. Our only challenge was figuring out how to get our lunch up to the loft without any mishaps.

Damien looked at me with a mischievous grin. "I have an idea. Go over to the rope that's dangling outside the barn."

He scurried up the ladder as fast as he could. Following his request, I stood next to the rope. Suddenly, the loft door swung open, and he retrieved the rope. Damien momentarily disappeared for only a moment to reappear with a bale of hay secured to it.

"Heads up, Brian, I am going to lower this down, please place everything on the bale, and I will then hoist it back up."

I placed our meal on the bale of hay and looked up, then I pulled on the rope. "Alright, Damien, go ahead and pull."

I could not resist the temptation and decided to hop on the bale as it was being raised. Once we reached the top, Damien shot me a look.

"Brian, you cow, I should let go right now and drop you."

I just laughed. "I know, however, this was the quickest way up here."

Damien huffed in annoyance. "Very well, please wait a moment while I secure the rope, then I will pull you in."

Damien snatched a pole equipped with a hook on the end and grabbed the rope, pulling us closer to the ledge. I leaped off and retrieved our lunch and blankets. Afterward, Damien moved the bale of hay to the side.

We spread out the blankets on the hay-covered wooden floor, then lay down, resting for a bit in each other's arms. It was such a comfortable feeling lying next to Damien, not worrying about someone barging in on us. I pulled off my shirt and laid it behind us, and Damien did the same. We lay back down with his head resting on my chest as his hands delicately traveled over my body, tracing the line down to my navel. I gasped as I felt his breath against my chest. Once more, I found myself becoming aroused by every touch he made.

"Damien, you're doing it again."

He looked up at me with an expression of pure innocence until the moment his hand ventured a little too low, then quickly pulled back.

"Oh I'm sorry, I didn't mean to."

I laughed softly. "It is perfectly natural, considering the obvious mutual attraction between us. Nevertheless, I am cautious about rushing things and risking having any regrets. I want it to be special for both of us. While we have advanced to a certain level of intimacy, what our friends would call first base and perhaps progressing to second in the near future, I believe before we go all the way, we should both be ready. In the meantime, we may have to take a few cold showers or take care of business when we are home alone in bed at night."

Damien giggled. "I don't think Mrs. Crabtree would approve of that."

"What she does not know will not hurt her. Besides, we are guys, and it is something that we just need to do from time to time."

"Alright, all this talk about sex is getting me aroused, so maybe we should change the subject and focus on a different topic, like eating something."

"That's an excellent suggestion; let me just grab the food."

We sat upright and indulged in the sandwiches we had prepared. Damien had a smudge of mustard on the corner of his lip. I gently wiped it away with my thumb before inserting it into my mouth. We opened the potato chips and drank the soda, consuming them completely. Then, Damien revealed two bars of chocolate that he had stashed, placing them beside the fruit. We then proceeded to feed each other.

"Damien, shall we talk about the dream I had this morning? It involved the night you left the house. While many of the details remain hazy, I can still recall the images of the warehouse illuminated by the candles. In the midst of this setting, a weird red-haired guy was engaged in a heated conversation with someone in a dark cloak; both were arguing about you until they noticed I was coming around, and they approached me, at which point, that's when I woke up. I don't know what it means, and it's frustrating that I can't remember more."

Damien put his arms around me in an attempt to comfort me. "It will be alright, Brian; just give it some time. We can talk with Matt once he gets back. He may know more about the situation. He believes they might be repressed memories from that evening. Rushing to confront their memories might be too painful. "Therefore, let's see what he has to say before taking any further action."

"You are probably right. So what are we supposed to do until he gets home?"

Damien flashed me a devilish grin. "What did you say about first base and rolling in the hay?"

I knew how to take a hint and moved closer to Damien, giving him a big, passionate kiss.

Chapter Seven
Damian

As we lay back, I tried to conceal my fear of being alone that kept creeping into my thoughts, and I had to keep reminding myself that I needed to stop worrying so much. I knew this situation was not going to last forever, as Brian would be going away in a year or so, yet I could not help but wonder if all this was worth it.

I never really had the opportunity to make any real friends, after having been moved from house to house throughout the years. However, right now, this feels truly wonderful as I looked into his eyes while he lay beside me. I guess it is better to cherish these moments with each other than to never have experienced them at all. I need to stop worrying about the future, because who knows what tomorrow will bring?

Brian gently nudged and asked, "Hey Damien, what are you thinking about? For a moment there, you looked like you were miles away."

I merely glanced back at him and smiled. "I am fine, just thinking about our relationship and how great it feels being with you like this."

"So am I, my sweet, so am I."

After we ate our lunch, talked some more, and played around for hours, we lost track of time when unexpectedly Matt's head popped up from the ladder.

In a sarcastic manner, Matt called out, "I'm coming up. Are you boys decent?"

Out of reflex, we both attempted to cover ourselves. Fortunately, we were still wearing our pants.

"Matt, you perv, you scared the crap out of us. How did you know that we were out here anyway?"

"You think I have not made out in the barn on several occasions throughout the years? Nevertheless, considering all the doors were open, I presumed that someone was probably out here."

My eyes widened, and I hurled an empty soda can in his direction. Matt slid down the ladder laughing.

"You're lucky I missed."

Matt simply smiled and said, "Once you boys are finished playing around, please come into the house, and we can discuss what we are going to have for dinner."

"Very well, we shall be down shortly."

Brian and I perched on the edge of the loft, our feet dangling as we gazed out over the horizon.

"Damien, I wish we could stay up here throughout the night. I imagine the view of the sunset is spectacular from up here, and I really do not want to sleep alone tonight. I do not mean in a romantic way; I would feel more comfortable if you were by my side in the event of another dream."

"Since we have a break from school for the next two days, I am sure that Matt would be willing to let you stay over. However, he will need to convince Mrs. Crabtree that it is alright."

"Well, it certainly would not hurt to ask. Let's clean up and go in to see what Matt has to say."

We put the trash in the center of one of the blankets, then I instructed Brian to go down the ladder and I would toss it down to him. He motioned for me to join him. I just could not resist the temptation to show off just a bit. So I turned around and leaped off the hayloft, landing on my feet like a cat. Then I ran around to Brian and tapped him on the shoulder, causing him to whip around, his eyes widened in surprise.

" How did you manage to get down here so fast?"

"I just jumped down from the loft, I do it all the time."

Brian simply shook his head in disbelief. "You are lucky you didn't break anything."

"It is nothing. I am young, and everyone thinks I am part cat. I always land on my feet."

Brian collected our stuff and looked at me intently. "If you say so." He murmured.

We proceeded toward the house and entered the kitchen, where Matt was talking with someone on the phone. From what I could overhear from fragments of the conversation, it became apparent that he was talking to Pat.

"Tell Pops I asked how it is going."

Matt chuckled. "Pat says hi and to not call him Pops."

We set our stuff down and threw away our trash before settling onto the sofa. Matt finished his phone conversation and entered the living room.

"I briefed Pat on Brian's dreams and recent events. He recommended that if the situation persists, we should seek advice from individuals we know who are better equipped to handle such matters."

"That's what Brian and I wanted to discuss with you. We were wondering whether it would be alright if Brian stayed overnight while we slept out in the hayloft."

"Boys, do you think you are ready for that?"

Brian stopped Matt before he could misconstrue the situation. "It is not what you think. I would appreciate Damien being there in case I experience another dream tonight. Considering it is the weekend and there's no school on Monday."

Matt pondered for a moment. "I will need to contact Mrs. Crabtree and get her approval, but I agree that it would be better for you both to be together because of the nature of the dreams. It might be best if you stayed here."

Damien agreed. "She would probably approve if there was another responsible adult to supervise the both of us."

Matt nearly choked in amazement. "An responsible adult? I believe you may have mistaken me for my brother. Nonetheless, it might be a good idea to stay here not only for the night but for a few days to delve deeper into this matter. I shall contact Mrs. Crabtree to explain the situation. Should she agree, you may stay in the loft this evening. Before that, who is in the mood for pizza?"

Brian and I turned and looked at each other and smiled. "You know we are always in the mood for pizza."

"Yeah your usual, pepperoni and pineapple, just the way you boys like it."

Matt ordered the pizza and then contacted Mrs. Crabtree informing her of the situation. Since she was already slightly concerned earlier during breakfast, she agreed under the condition that she be kept informed of Brian's progress.

As Brian and Damien hugged and kissed each other in celebration, the sound of a horn emanated from the driveway—dinner was about to be served.

Chapter Eight
Damien

After dinner, Brian and I grabbed some sleeping bags and camping supplies from the utility room downstairs. We raided the kitchen again for some snacks and soda for later. We said goodnight to Matt and assured him that we would call out if we needed his assistance. Matt was going to leave his bedroom window open because it was on the same side as the front of the barn, allowing for a refreshing cross breeze on the pleasantly cool night.

We arrived just in time to witness the sun setting. After transferring all our belongings to the hayloft, we lit the space with battery-operated lanterns, strategically placing them around the loft. Although not as romantic as candles, it was for the best; we did not want the barn to go up in flames. We nestled by the edge of the loft, and I tenderly put my arms around Brian, intertwining our hands as we watched the sun gradually disappear beyond the vast landscape.

Before the last bit of light faded away, I turned to kiss Brian, and he returned my affection. I made my way down his neck, kissing and lightly biting him. Then I proceeded to nibble on his neck, knowing that I was probably going to leave a mark. Brian whispered and let out a gasp. I gazed into his captivating green eyes. Then he started to give me that same wonderful attention. Unexpectedly, however, he let out a yawn. Hastily concealing his mouth with his hand, then we froze, he then looked up at me with a smile.

I playfully said, "I hope I'm not boring you, my dear."

He chuckled. "Not at all, Damien. I simply have not had much sleep in the last few days. I am not sure how long I will be able to stay awake."

I laughed softly. "It is alright, I understand. I know you have not slept well lately. As long as we are together, that is all I need to be happy."

"Perhaps we should make ourselves more comfortable and set up our sleeping bags. We can hold each other until I drift off to sleep."

I nodded in agreement. "I hope you do not mind that I prefer to sleep in my underwear, I do not like pajamas except when it is cold in the winter."

He offered me a sheepish grin. "No, not at all, that would be great with me."

After turning down our sleeping bags, we proceeded to take off our clothes. When Brian removed his shorts, I could not resist sneaking a peek. Then I proceeded to do the same, gradually easing out of my jeans. When I bent over, I noticed that Brian was also checking out my butt. I smiled warmly as he blushed and turned away.

We both settled into our sleeping bags, using the bales of hay as a makeshift headboard. I suggested that he recline against me since he seemed likely to fall asleep first. To my surprise, fueled by the soda he had consumed during our conversation, he managed to stay awake to talk and look out over the stars. However, his resolve was soon defeated. I tenderly smiled, planting a kiss on top of his head, and watched over him as he slept peacefully.

After an hour, I succumbed to the same fate and fell asleep. For a few hours, all was still and quiet, but in the wee hours of the morning, Brian began to whisper and talk in his sleep, and his body began to shake and twitch. It took a few minutes for me to wake from my own restful sleep. But as Brian's dreams intensified, I was alerted to the situation. It took a minute or two for me to come to my senses and realize that Brian was in the middle of another nightmare. My initial impulse was to wake him up, but considering he was reenacting that dreadful night in his dreams, I thought it best to leave him be—even if he ended up remembering what I am.

Brian had to navigate through this situation at his own pace. I stood by, observing and comforting him, anticipating the moment he would wake up. It appeared that it wouldn't be too much longer now. Brian's breathing and movements became more intense, ending in a sudden gasp followed by a piercing scream as he sat upright. Despite my attempts to comfort him, Brian momentarily pushed me away, disoriented and unsure of his surroundings. Eventually, Brian regained his composure.

There was a voice outside the barn, and Matt asked, "Is everything alright?" The screaming must have woken him up.

I responded, "Everything is fine. Brian just had another dream."

Matt told us that he would be right up. I rubbed Brian's shoulders, then he turned and hugged me and started to sob.

"Oh Damien, it was so terrible. There was so much more about that night that no one told me."

I gazed upon his sad face and wiped away his tears. "Hush, everything will be alright. He can't hurt either of us anymore; it is just a dream."

Matt popped up from the ladder, still in his bathrobe. "Are you boys decent, nothing I shouldn't see?"

We both chuckled. "No, everything is good. Come on up."

Matt approached and settled on a bale of hay beside us. "Are you doing okay? Can you tell us what you remember?"

"I am fine, just a little shaken. What time is it?"

Damien glanced at his watch. "It's three a.m."

Matt touched his arm. "It's alright, take your time, we are not going anywhere."

Brian exhaled deeply. "Certain parts still remain a little foggy, yet I distinctly remember being back at the warehouse." It was really hard for me to think; I felt like I'd been drugged. My vision was blurry, and I could hear the voices of the two men engaged in a heated dispute concerning you, Damien. Someone in a dark cloak told the red-haired guy that he shouldn't have gotten involved and that it was going to get him killed. The red-haired man said he did not care and he never wanted to be like this. Then they must have eventually realized that I was coming around. They approached me for a closer look, and the individual in the cloak said there was something different about me, and I shouldn't be coming around already. I moaned and shifted my gaze to the side, where I saw a couple of kids lying on the sofa next to me. It looked like they were dead, and I screamed, and that's when I woke up. Oh god, it was terrible."

Brian began to weep once more, and I embraced him tightly. Matt knelt down next to Brian.

"Sorry we did not tell you about the homeless kids. We did not know how much you saw that night, and thought if any memory was there, it should come back on its own so you would not be so traumatized. The red-haired guy killed the kids and dumped them behind the building. There is still more to the story that you do not remember yet, such as what really happened to the red-haired guy that fateful evening. However, I do not think you are ready for it just yet."

Brian grabbed Matt. "But why couldn't I remember all this before?"

I was trying to comfort Brian the best I could.

Then Matt said, "Because the mind sometimes represses traumatic memories that we are not able to deal with, and even after you do remember everything, you may need some therapy to be able to deal with all of it."

"I wonder what they did to me and why they called me different."

I looked down and shook my head. "We don't know, and we may never know unless we find out who our mysterious friend in the hooded cloak is. Nevertheless, we will do our best to find out. I just hope, when this is all over, that you still feel the same way about me. Because there is something different about me too. I have been trying to think of a way to tell you, but now that the dreams have started, we think it better to wait until this is all over."

Brian cupped his hands around my face and looked me in the eye. "There is nothing that can change how I feel about you. There are other people that care about you—even Mrs. Crabtree finally came around." Then he kissed me.

Matt cleared his throat. "Alright, gentlemen, it appears that the time has come to conclude your romantic interlude for this evening. Since we are already awake, why don't we freshen up and go for an early breakfast? I will go ahead so I do not have to see you in your tighty-whities."

Chapter Nine
Damien

We all returned to the house to freshen up. Brian and I took the downstairs bathroom while Matt used the upstairs one. I pondered the idea of joining Brian in the shower, curious to see what he looked like without anything on. Although it wouldn't be so unusual for two boys to shower together—we do it in the foster homes to save on water and time. However, the thought of showering with Brian was a unique situation.

I will need to be patient and refrain from thinking about stuff like that because if I do not, I may not be able to control myself, and I am afraid everything will change between us after we do. What if I am really bad at it, and what if I suck? No pun intended.

I was so deep in thought that I failed to notice Brian had come out of the shower. His sudden touch on my shoulder startled me momentarily. It struck me then, what kind of a vampeal was I to allow someone to sneak up on me so easily? Yet, Brian was not just anyone, I guess.

"Sorry, Damien the shower is all yours."

I smiled and blushed, attempting to conceal the evident arousal I was sporting.

"Thank you, I will be ready in a few minutes."

Then I hurried into the bathroom, dropping my towel and stepping into the shower. A yelp escaped my lips as I turned the knob to the cold water, bracing myself hoping that would do the trick.

Brian popped his head into the bathroom. "You alright?"

I was still attempting to conceal myself. "Yes, I'm fine, I forgot to adjust the water temperature."

Brian giggled softly. "That trick works but not for very long. Trust me, I have put it to the test ." with that, he gracefully disappeared behind the door.

Oh my god, is he trying to drive me crazy? Both of us are aware of each other's desires,but are we prepared to act upon the fantasies that only we dream about at night when we are alone? Will he feel the same after he finds out that I am a vampeal, or will he think I am a monster just like the red-haired vampire said?

Okay Damien, get out of your freaking head and stop worrying about something that has not happened yet. I shut off the water and drew back the shower curtain, proceeding to dry myself off. Stepping out into the hallway where Brian was waiting, already dressed.

"Do you feel better now?"

I smiled and embraced him, feeling a little annoyed because Brian was right—it did not last for long. However, it does not take that much to get excited either. I led Brian by hand to the upstairs bedroom, where we could get dressed. I selected a snug t-shirt and a pair of jeans that were always one size too small, so they would accentuate everything.

I turned to Brian and saw him staring at me. "Okay mister, no show for you, turn around."

Brian gave me a pouty expression but did as I asked. Despite his attempt to sneak a peek, I noticed his reflection in the mirror adjacent to the door. Once finished, we went downstairs where Matt was waiting for us.

"Excellent, you are ready. I was beginning to wonder if the two of you were going to start something, leaving me waiting downstairs all morning."

I looked over at Brian and winked before returning back to Matt. "Oh, the thought did cross our minds."

Matt chuckled. "Yeah, you two are always thinking about it."

That's when I blushed again because we couldn't deny it.

The three of us went out to the truck, and we saw a magnificent sight of the sun rising over the hill. It was then I felt Brian's tender kiss upon my cheek.

I turned and smiled. "What was that for?"

"For just being you."

Matt cleared his throat. "Alright love-birds, hop in the truck. You are starting to make me feel a little jealous."

Brian climbed in first, sliding over to Matt, and just as he got in he smacked a big kiss on the side of Matt's face. We all paused for a moment, then we busted up laughing.

Matt shook his head. "You goddamn kids are going to drive me crazy."

Matt put the truck in gear, and we were off. We arrived at Denny's, where we were greeted by a waitress sporting a blonde bouffant hairdo, wearing a brown and yellow dress with multicolored stripes, seating us at a table in the back corner, with a lit cigarette hanging from her lips.

"What can I get you gentlemen to drink?"

Matt just requested a coffee, and Brian and I asked for large orange juices. The waitress left to get our drinks. Brian brought up the subject of the dream first.

"Guys, what do you think all this means? Why can't I remember the rest?"

Matt glanced in my direction and remarked, "You are definitely beginning to remember the events of that night. I am certain there is more to the story. Only Damien and Pat can fill in the gaps, but as I previously mentioned, it would not be wise to press the matter. The dreams are gradually revealing the information slowly so your mind has time to process the trauma of the ordeal. I believe it will not be much longer now before everything is clear."

Brian lowered his head. "This is driving me crazy. Did that guy really kill those kids, and was I next?"

I gently touched Brian's arm, attempting to get his attention, but the waitress arrived with our drinks and asked if we knew what we wanted or if we needed a few more minutes. Brian ordered a grand slam, I went for the same; while Matt opted for three eggs sunny side up and a side of toast. Taking a sip of my orange juice, we continued our conversation, Brian's hand gently resting on mine.

"I do not think he was going to kill you, at least not right then. He was using you as bait to lure me out. I encountered him at the park before he found you the following night. There are additional details, but I am unsure how much you saw or not. I cannot tell you now, but I think you should remember most of it in the next night or two at the rate you're going. I simply hope you feel the same after you know everything."

Brian kissed me. "As I previously told you before, of course I will feel the same. Why wouldn't I?"

Now it was my turn to lower my head. "Like I said, there are a few things that you don't know about me."

Brian glanced over at Matt then shifted back at me. "Matt, are you familiar with the subject Damien is referring to? You do not have to tell me what it is right now. But do you and Pat have any issues with it?"

"No, not at all—but it might be a little strange."

Brian smirked. "I traveled all over the world with my parents before they died and have seen lots of strange things in my time. If

Matt and Pat aren't bothered by it, then everything should be fine. Also, I haven't been able to tell you everything about me either. We all have a few things that we do not share with anyone until the time is right. You know that I have to leave after I turn eighteen, and it is not just because I will be aging out of the foster home. I have to go back home and don't have any choice in the matter. It is not something I can talk about right now either. Knowing that I have to leave, I would understand if you don't want to be my boyfriend anymore."

"Don't be silly, I already knew you were planning to go, and if you cannot talk about it now, I will, of course, respect it."

Matt interrupted by clearing his throat. "Brian, I am somewhat curious about what you previously said. You recollected in your dream encountering someone in a dark cloak, who mentioned there was something special about you. Damien and Pat did not say anything about someone else being there."

Damien shook his head. "No, we did not encounter anyone besides the red-haired guy."

Matt arched his eyebrow. " Perhaps he was hiding somewhere in the shadows watching. Brian, do you know what they are talking about?"

"No, not particularly. I may be well off financially, but other than that, I'm just like anyone else."

Matt thought for a moment. "When Pat gets back in a day or two, I am going to see if the authorities have any ideas about this."

I glanced towards the waitress as she approached our table with our order. "Perfect timing, let's dig in. I'm starving."

Chapter Ten
Brian

Damien, Matt, and I returned to their house a few hours later. We needed to decide how to spend our Sunday.

I looked over at Damien with a smile. "So what do you want to do today—more playing around in the barn, or did you have something else in mind?"

Damien turned and paused, then thought for a second. "We should not waste our entire weekend in the barn, although that does sound like fun. Perhaps jogging down by the river and then maybe heading over to the mall and catching a movie would be a worthwhile plan. Let's check the current movie listings to see what is playing today. Matt, you should come with us."

Matt laughed. "Not really into the whole running thing, and I think you two should savor your long weekend together. I need to call Pat and Mrs. Crabtree and give them an update. Hopefully, this will be over soon, and you will be able to sleep at night again, Brian."

I nodded my head in agreement. "I'm ready for this to be over with. After what I remembered last night, I feel a bit frightened, but I know they are just pictures in my mind. Maybe tonight we can sleep in Damien's room."

Damien started to say something, but Matt cut him off.

"Damien's bed is too small. Why don't you two sleep in Pat's room tonight? He has that giant king-size bed."

I glanced towards Damien and inquired, "Do you think it will be alright with Pat?"

Matt simply shrugged his shoulders. "I am sure it will be fine since he is not here right now, and it is only for a few nights. Now if I were my strict twin brother, I might feel compelled to remind you boys to behave. However, I know you guys will do what your heart tells you to, no matter what we say."

Damien looked at his uncle and blushed. I wrapped my arms around Damien and gently addressed Matt, " We have not yet reached that stage in our relationship. Since it will be the first time for both of us, we want to make it special. Perhaps around Damien's sixteenth birthday. Furthermore, if we were going to proceed, it wouldn't matter if there was a bed or not."

Damien shoved me, causing me to stumble a little, while Matt simply laughed. "Well, you got me there, kid. If your determination is strong enough, you will find a place. You boys should get going."

I looked over at Damien and nodded in agreement. "You are right, we should go for our run then come back and take a shower before getting ready for the movie."

We swiftly made it down to the river in no time. Following our jog, we paused by the river's edge to rest for a moment and looked out over the water that connected Ohio to Kentucky.

Damien turned to me. "Brian, do you really truly believe we can keep our hands off each other for that long? It seems to be such a long time away."

I simply smiled. "I do not know, considering I have waited this long. Without a doubt, there will be a lot of cold showers and plenty of solitary indulgence at night, but I really want you to be ready. In any case, when I was overseas, I saw two guys engaging in such an activity. It was passionate, but I thought it would be very uncomfortable the first time if you do not know what you are doing."

Damien giggled. "I know what you mean. I have seen some pictures and read some of the stories in Matt's magazines that he has hidden in his bedroom. I sneak them out sometimes when he is out of town. I am not sure I can do some of the things that they talk about."

Well, that certainly piqued my interest. "Matt has dirty magazines stashed in his bedroom? You will have to show me where he hides them. Are there lots of pictures?"

"Yes, but we should change the subject… It is going to make our run that much harder otherwise."

I could tell that Damien was getting a little excited and was starting to blush again. "Alright, I will race you to the park at the end."

I took off, trying to get a head start, yet Damien effortlessly kept up with me. As we neared the park, I exerted myself, trying to get there before Damien. However, he was still faster than me and got there first, but only by a few seconds. Collapsing onto a park bench, I gasped for air, trying to catch my breath, while it seemed like Damien was just barely unaffected by the exertion. He circled around me and taunted me.

"I was slightly perturbed"Damien, nobody likes a show-off, you know."

He simply laughed. "Very well, please have a seat and let us take a moment to rest for a bit. How much of that evening do you remember thus far?"

"Well, I recall feeling deeply bad about what happened the night Mrs. Crabtree kicked you out. Prior to that incident, I never told anyone about being gay except for you. Therefore, I got really scared when she walked in on us. Later, after talking with Pat, I decided to help look for you. Upon reaching the river, I asked everyone I could find if they remembered seeing someone with your description, but no luck.

It was getting dark, so I decided to rest at the park here and think about what to do. After a while, I started to sense that someone was watching me. I looked around, but despite my efforts, I did not see anyone. It made me feel a little uneasy, and I was about to leave when the red-haired guy just popped out of nowhere. He scared the heck out of me because I had no idea where he came from. I started to leave, but he stopped me and asked what I was doing out here all alone. I told him I was looking for a friend. It was getting late, and it was time to come home. He proceeded to describe you and mentioned your name. He told me you were staying at the warehouse with some other kids from off the street to get out of the rain.

Well, stupid me, I instructed him to take me to you right away so I could tell you I was sorry. We got back to the warehouse and down to the storeroom, and that was when everything went black. The details still remain hazy in my dreams. I wanted to get out of there so badly, yet I found I could not move, and I remembered that he said you were there. I was worried about what he had done to you. That is when I blacked out once more, only to be roused by the sound of your voice followed by Pat's. I know the rest is important, but I cannot remember."

Damien wrapped his arms around me and planted a tender kiss on my cheek. "You will, my dear, and we will be there by your side when you do."

I grinned. "I know you will. However in the meantime, let us think of something more fun to do."

Chapter Eleven
Damien

When we returned to the house, we cleaned up. I beat Brian with ease—he was a little annoyed about it, although he didn't know I was holding back a little. Even without feeding to give me super-speed, being a vampeal still had its perks. Perhaps one day, I let him win—maybe. As we entered the living room and settled on the sofa, Matt was in the kitchen engaging in a conversation on the telephone with someone. Then he hung up and came into the living room with us.

"So boys, how was the run?"

I laughed. "It was great, I beat Brian home again."
Brian huffed. "I can't help that you're such a speed demon, it's just not natural."

My eyes widened, and I looked at Matt. Though I understood that Brian was just kidding, I was still a little scared about revealing the truth to him.

I just gave a defensive laugh. "Don't beat yourself up about it, babe. I've been running down by that river every day for years. Nonetheless, it was nice we got to talk things through. By the way, Matt, who were you talking to on the phone?"

"That was my brother. I was updating him on the situation. He mentioned he should be back home tomorrow and is stopping by the office to see Mr. Craft. Pat also suggested that Brian might consider consulting with Damien's therapist after he remembers everything." Brian grabbed my arm. "I didn't know you were seeing a therapist, Damien."

I nodded to confirm Matt's statement. "It's just once a week. They simply wanted to make sure that I am coping with everything that happened. I believe we were all somewhat shaken up after that night."

"Well if you think seeing a therapist will help... I'm not sure how Mrs. Crabtree will take it."

Matt approached Brian and gently placed his hand on his shoulder. "I am sure she will be fine once we talk to her and let her know what is going on and explain the situation. By the way, I have got some errands to run. Are you guys still heading over to the mall?"

I looked at Brian and grinned. "Yes, we can get something to eat there and do a little shopping as well. Later, we were thinking that we would go to the drive-in for a double feature. "They have a special showing for Labor Day weekend."

Matt thought for a moment before giving us a sly smirk. "I have a hunch about what you are going to see, and I am not sure whether Pat or Mrs. Crabtree would approve. However, if anyone asks, you just went to see a movie at the mall. You might want to take a look at the current movie listings there, just in case someone asks what you saw. That's what I would do. Nevertheless, if you get caught, I will deny everything I told you."

Brian and I agreed. With that, Matt was out the kitchen door and on his way. Brian and I got all cleaned up and changed our clothes before heading off in Brian's car to the mall.

We shopped at several of the clothing stores for a while. Well, Brian did most of the shopping because he gets a generous allowance from his trust fund each month. My budget only accommodated a shirt and a pair of jeans. Afterwards we decided to take a break and get something to eat at the food court. We kept debating over hamburgers or Chinese food—hamburgers won out this time with a large order of fries and a milkshake.

We eventually arrived at the arcade and dumped massive amounts of quarters into our favorite game machines, such as Space Invaders and Tetris. We engaged in a friendly competition to see who was the best. I killed him at Space Invaders, but he got me on Tetris. Before we knew it, time had slipped away, and we realized that we had been playing for hours, and it was time to go. After dropping off all our purchases at home, we proceeded to the drive-in.

"So Brian, this is our first drive-in together."

He smiled. "Yep, just like a real couple."

The woman at the ticket booth cast a disapproving glance before taking our money, gesturing for us to proceed. Brian found a secluded spot off to the side where there didn't seem to be too many cars. He rolled down the window most of the way and grabbed the silver box speaker that was attached to the nearby pole, placing it on the edge of the window. We reclined our seats, waiting for the movie to start on the one-hundred-foot screen.

I sighed and turned to Brian. "But are we, like, a real couple? Yes, I know we're dating each other, but we can't go around school holding hands and kissing each other like other teenagers our age. Nobody knows we're gay, and we don't have any other friends. Can you handle it if our classmates find out? You already freaked out on me once with Mrs. Crabtree. Will you still be there if they find out and start talking about us behind our backs?"

Then it was Brian's turn to sigh. "I suppose that is a valid question considering my actions that night, and I understand how you might be worried. Pat and Matt mentioned that life will get better after high school and that we will meet other people like us. They're probably already talking about us because we're different, and they think we are the sad little orphan kids. It's just a lot easier if we hide it from them right now. I do not believe that there is anyone who needs to know anyway. We have support from the people that really matter already.

By the way, when did you start worrying about what people thought about you? You are always so confident in everything you do."

"No, not always. I'm just good at not showing it. There are some people that I care very much about what they think of me."

I slid closer to Brian and jumped suddenly as a Pink Panther cartoon started playing on the screen and blasting over the speaker. Brian promptly lowered the volume, then turned to me.

" Damien, I will get us some sodas from the concession stand." After he left, I just sat back and watched the rest of the cartoon. Moments later, there was a tap on the window, startling me once more. Brian had returned with a tray of sodas and a big tub of popcorn. I rolled the window down, took it from him, and sat it on the seat between us.

Then Brian got back in the car and just smiled at me."Damien, I understand it won't always be easy, but in time, I believe it will be better."

I reached for his hand, and he pulled me close and gave me a kiss before sitting back as the movie started. We laughed a lot throughout "Flesh Gordon." The movie was so funny and cheesy with lots of people running around nude because they were turned on by a sex ray. Flesh, with the help of Dale and Dr. Jerkoff, had to save the planet from Emperor Wang. In spite of all that, there were some special effects that were kind of cool.

After the first movie, there was a brief ten-minute intermission allowing everyone to go to the restroom or get some more refreshments. Brian excused himself and went to take a leak, while I got us more popcorn, hot dogs for both of us, and two more sodas. Brian made it back before I did, so I handed him the food and made a mad dash for the restroom before the second feature.

I returned just as they started to play Barbarella—it was also slightly cheesy but not as bad and had far less nudity. The one thing I loved seeing was Pygar the angel. He was strikingly handsome, and if I had any doubts about my sexuality, they were gone now. I so wanted to be Jane Fonda at that moment.

After the movies ended, all the cars started leaving. We sat there for a few minutes letting them pass. Brian disposed of our trash in the designated bins and hung the speaker back on the stand. Pretty much everyone had left when Brian reached over to pull me close. Before leaving, we shared one final kiss before heading home. I sighed, so content with myself after our fabulous date.

Chapter Twelve
Brian

Damien and I arrived back at his house slightly late, finding that Matt had already gone to bed. We quietly went to Pat's bedroom and turned on the light. We both went over to the bed and sat down, with Damien on the right and me on the left.

I turned to Damien and reached for his hand. "I guess we better try to get some sleep."

We pulled back the covers. Damien and I got undressed, both of us stealing a little peek at each other before modesty prompted us to turn away once we were down to our underwear. Then we got in bed, pulling the soft and plush quilt up and making ourselves comfortable. Damien laid his head on my chest, gazing up at me with those beautiful lavender eyes.

"You can rest assured that I will be here for you the entire time, and always remember—it is just a dream, and nothing can harm you. It is your dream and you're in control."

I let out a deep sigh. "I know, Damien. I just wish I could bring you into my dream with me."

I could see Damien grin. "Well, in a way, I am. You know that I am going to come for you, so when you see my T-shirt, let it serve as a reminder that it is a dream and that I am coming to find you and will be there soon."

I smiled warmly and planted a gentle kiss on his forehead. Exhaustion had taken over at this point. I could not stay awake any longer, and soon I got the sensation that I was floating on air just above the bed. Suddenly, I jerked and out of nowhere felt my body crash back down onto the bed. It startled me for a second. I looked around the room only to find Damien was not there next to me on the bed; the door to the bedroom was open, and there was a light in the hallway.

I rose out of bed and figured that Damien was unable to sleep either—perhaps due to having eaten so much junk food at the drive-in. I stepped into the hallway, and the lights got so intense that I had to shield my eyes with my hand; then everything went black. Eventually, my eyes adjusted to the light in a very dimly lit room, with only a few candles for illumination.

I found myself back at the warehouse and noticed Damien's t-shirt was left on the sofa. Then I recalled what Damien told me—that this was my dream and I was in control. I turned, and that's when the red-haired man popped out of the shadows and took me by the hand, leading me to the sofa. Standing very close, I could feel his icy breath on the side of my face, sending shivers down my spine. I wanted him to stop and leave me alone, but I was powerless to stop him. I thought he was going to kiss me as he brushed past my lips but then moved down to my neck, where he bit down. Initially there was a sharp pain, then it felt soothing and warm. That is when everything went fuzzy. Just then, a figure stopped him, effortlessly tossing the man across the room, slamming him against the far wall, and collapsing to the floor. It was the individual in the dark cloak. They were arguing about something.

But that's when I lost consciousness for a few minutes or so. I could hear voices, and that's when I overheard them talk about Damien and how this was only going to get the red-haired guy killed. I glanced over to the other sofa and noticed the kids lying stiff and motionless. I wanted to let out a piercing scream but found myself unable to do so. It was at that moment when both the red-haired and cloaked figure turned their attention towards me and noticed that I was coming around. The man with the red hair said there was something different about me, claiming that he could tell when he tasted my blood.

But the hooded figure stopped and briefly paused for a moment to listen before turning around. "Damien is here." In a split second, they vanished, then it went dark again until I started to hear Damien and Pat's voices. I attempted to call out, but I couldn't. I didn't have the strength.

Finally I could see the three of them engaged in a heated argument. I tried to figure out what was happening. The red-haired guy lunged toward Pat, but not before Damien hit him really hard across the face. In a fit of rage, the guy redirected his attention back toward Damien, hissing. I heard a loud crash, and Pat broke off a table leg that was located to the left of me. I was frozen as I just watched Pat dig the leg into his back. The red-haired guy swiftly turned back toward him, and I could now see he had fangs like a wild animal. That's also when I got a better view of Damien as well—he appeared to have claws and fangs too—before he jabbed his fist into the guy's chest, then the red-haired guy decayed and burst into flames.

I blacked out again until I heard Damien's voice; he was gently shaking me, telling me to wake up. Gradually, the voice was getting louder, prompting me to open my eyes. I realized Damien was sitting next to me, and that I was back in Pat's bedroom, and the dream was over. I smiled and gave him a big hug and kissed him.

Damien pulled back slightly. "Brian, are you alright?"

I embraced him once more. "Yes, I am fine. I think I know everything now."

Damien looked concerned. "What do you mean by everything?"

"Regarding the red-haired vampire and even what you are, or **at least** what I think you are. I do **not** know why it happened, yet I do know both of you saved me, and that I **am** not frightened of you."

Damien scratched his head. "Well, there are some details that I probably need to clarify, but I am pleased that we can talk about it now."

There was a tap on the door, and Matt poked his head into the room. "You boys alright?"

"Yes, come on in, we're just talking."

Matt came over and sat on the edge of the bed. "Brian, did you have another dream?"

I nodded my head. "Yes, and I think I remember pretty much everything now. I saw Damien and Pat saving me from the vampire, and I suspect Damien is one too. However, I am wondering how you are able to go out in sunlight, or is that just a myth?"

Damien giggled. "Well, I am only half-vampire, a vampeal to be precise. I am not one of the living dead, nor a bloodsucker. I do feed, but I consume life energy through my fingertips, and my fangs are mostly for show. Matt and Pat belong to an organization known as the Feral Society. They assist kids with special abilities, such as myself, to fit into society.

I am sorry the vampire got you involved. He was upset with me that night because I interrupted his dinner, and he confronted me in the park. I was already in a foul mood after getting kicked out of the house, and you kinda bailing on me. The vampire tried to attack me, but I managed to break his arm. He ran away, and I hoped that was the end of it. I hid downstairs in that warehouse, and that's where you came in later."

I just looked at Damien. Momentarily speechless at first, then I started to laugh so hard that it caused me to fall off the bed, tumbling on the floor. Both Damien and Matt rushed over to help me up, with very concerned looks on their faces.

Damien expressed, "Well, that is not the reaction I was expecting. God, I hope I did not break something."

Then Matt added, "Brian, are you alright?"

I finally regained my composure and took a deep breath. Tears streamed down my face, and I felt a stitch in my side. "Yes, oh yes, sorry about that; however, as I mentioned before, you are not the only one with a secret."

Damien flashed a smile at me. "You mentioned that the figure in the cloak and the vampire sensed there was something different about you. Are you supernatural?"

I shook my head and walked over to my backpack. I pulled out a little leather pouch.

Matt's eyes widened. "Is that…?"

But before anyone said another word, I took a pinch of the powder and sprinkled it over me. In an instant, I effortlessly floated towards the ceiling. "No, I'm not really supernatural; I am entirely human. This is pixie dust, and I'm one of the Lost Boys from Neverland."

Damien and Matt both simultaneously sat back on the bed, their mouths gaping. I descended back down to the floor and went to sit beside them.

"Well, I suppose it is my turn to ask you guys if you are alright. Damien, you are not the only one being looked after by the Feral

Society. I also have my own Renfield. I returned from Neverland two years ago to grow up and hoped to find someone to love. However there is one catch."

Damien wrapped his arms around me. "You cannot stay, which is why you have to go back, isn't it?"

"Yes, once I turn eighteen, but that's a long story. Anyway, it is four o'clock in the morning. Perhaps we can still get a few more hours of sleep before I get into the rest of the story."

They both agreed, and Damien turned to me. "Do you think you'll be able to sleep better now?"

Matt walked over to the door and said, "I believe you both should rest easier now that the cat's out of the bag, more or less. I think the vampire tried to compel you, but it did not work as he planned. Perhaps due to the pixie dust, who knows. Your mind was resisting his influence all this time, and now you know the truth, it should be better now."

Matt went back to his room, and Damien and I got back into bed, pulled the blanket around us, and turned off the light.

Chapter Thirteen
Brian

I awoke to the most delightful scent of something being prepared in the kitchen. glancing over, I determined that Damien was still sleeping. Very carefully, I slipped out of bed and put on some shorts and a t-shirt. Soon after, I noticed Damien stirring as he stretched, then he proceeded to get dressed himself.

"How did you sleep, Brian?"

"A lot better than I have in a long time. What is that wonderful smell? It appears that someone is already making breakfast."

I smiled. "Well, let's not keep them waiting, I am starving."

We discovered Matt in an apron and his boxer shorts, preparing delectable stacks of pancakes. He had already arranged two plates on the table, accompanied by glasses of freshly squeezed orange juice for us.

I grinned. "Fortunately, we did not have to work for our breakfast like at the foster home."

Matt laughed. "I am certain there is something I can delegate for you boys to do around here. Or, I could inquire with Mrs. Crabtree if she requires any assistance."

I glanced over at Damien, and we shook our heads. "No, that is okay, we are fine."

Matt grinned. "Would you gentlemen care to take a seat at the kitchen table? I shall promptly bring the pancakes over, after which we can finish our conversation from last night."

He didn't have to ask us twice. Within seconds, we had already started to chow down on breakfast.

I looked at Matt. "Aren't you going to join us?"

"I am good. I already ate while I was cooking. I am fine with my coffee; you guys just finished up now."

Matt placed his cup in the sink and rinsed it off before heading into the living room. A few minutes later, Damien and I followed and joined him. Damien and I settled on the sofa, where I put my arms around him, while Matt occupied the recliner positioned off to the side. Our calm setting was disrupted by the sound of the back door opening before Pat came through the kitchen.

Damien rose from his seat and gave him a warm hug. " It is nice to have you back."

Matt grinned. "Indeed, glad to see you back home, and the timing could not be better—Brian had another dream last night, recalling pretty much everything. We were just about to discuss it. He remembered how both of you defended yourselves against the vampire and that Damien is a vampeal. We told him about the Feral Society and our relationship with them. Furthermore, we recently discovered that Brian, much like Damien, is also under the watchful eye of the Feral Society, making him far from an ordinary boy."

Damien noticed that Pat had a little grin on his face. "You are not surprised at all. Did you know about this?"

Pat was still smiling. "No, I just discovered it myself this morning when I went to present Mr. Craft with my report on another one of my other kids. I must say, Brian, you look great for your age. However, this is not my story to tell, so why don't you enlighten us with the rest of it?"

I blushed and attempted to articulate my thoughts. " I previously mentioned that I am one of the lost boys and lived in Neverland. I stopped aging forty years ago when Peter found me after the tragic death of my parents. After their passing, I lived with my grandmother for a while."

Damien's eyes widened in astonishment. "Wait, if you lived with your grandmother forty years ago, that would make her…"

"Indeed, she passed away a considerable time ago. Upon my return two years ago, I lived with my aunt, who is my mother's sister, yet I told everyone that she was my grandmother—it simplified matters. I also have a half-sister who is still alive. My father was a bit of a playboy when he was young, engaging in a relationship with both my mother and my aunt, among others. Eventually, he decided to settle down and married my mother, but not before he managed to get both of them pregnant. My sister, who is slightly older than me, and I were designated as co-heirs to my father's estate upon his passing. During my absence, she oversaw the management of my father's business."

Pat shifted his weight slightly, standing in the hallway, with an interesting look on his face.

"Brian, Mr. Craft has only provided me with limited details regarding your background, and there is something that I suspect about your name. The Feral Society allowed Damien to choose his own name when he was younger. I am curious if the name you arrived at the foster home with is your given name?"

Damien's eyes widened, and he began to say something in response.

I put my hand on Damien's thigh. "It is all right, and it is a valid question. When I returned from Neverland, I used my mother and aunt's maiden name, Middleton, as my last name. However, my true family surname is Forestone."

Matt was beaming with excitement. "You are the elusive heir to the Forestone fortune. The young charge under my care came across mention of you during my time at the university in Florida. Reports have suggested that nobody has seen you since the tragic loss of your family."

Brian smiled. "I didn't really want anything to do with it. I had a hard time grieving their loss, and Peter came to me and said that he could take all the pain away."

Pat now displayed a look of concern on his face. "Could he do that? I did not think that was possible."

Brian sighed. "Yes and no. Regrettably, I was unable to fly to Neverland unaided. Peter had to accompany me because I could not think of any happy thoughts. However, after I was there, Peter possessed a remarkable ability to show you things that make you forget all your worries. He makes you feel like you can be a kid forever and never grow old, never get sick, or die. Yet, there is only one kid that never grows up, and that is Peter Pan.

After I was able to process the grief of losing my parents, I would return once a year on the anniversary of their passing to be with my sister and my aunt, but eventually every lost boy yearns for more and wants to find someone to fall in love with."

Matt had a puzzled look on his face. "Are some of the lost boys girls like Wendy?"

Brian smiled. "Yes, but like Wendy, they do not stay as long because they want to start a family a lot sooner than most of the boys. There have been a few lesbian girls who managed to stay a little longer, but they finally also leave."

Damien placed his hand on my thigh. "You mentioned that you have to go when you turn eighteen."

I turned to him and grasped his hand gently. "Yes, I cannot stay. Once I turn eighteen, I will start to age more rapidly. The manner of the aging process is different for every individual, but we all start to age unless we return to Neverland. Regrettably, I cannot go back to Peter and the Lost Boys, leaving those of us who have outgrown childhood to seek refuge at one of the other lands encircling Neverland. Some join the pirates, while others choose to live in the quaint villages or towns scattered across the island. As for myself, I shall be going to an island known as Elsewhere situated on the fringes of Neverland. It is filled with a diverse array of young men and women who can live their lives the way they want to, without the fear of anyone judging them for being different."

"That sounds wonderful, perhaps I could join you," Damien remarked.

Pat shook his head. "Not everyone can live in Neverland. Most supernatural beings are unable to linger for very long; the environment has an adverse effect and they become ill."

"I would love to stay and be with you, Damien; however, as you see, I cannot. If you want to call off what we have, I will be crushed but I understand."

Damien sighed. " You know, life can really suck. And here I was concerned that you might not accept me because I am a vampeal. Now

I find myself facing a decision to break my heart now, or do it later when you have to leave. Though I will probably regret this, I think I want to make the most of the time that we have left together."

Then Damien and I embraced once more, and I gave him a tender kiss.

Damien turned and looked at me. "You can fly with that dust you used—will it work on me as well?"

Brian pondered for a second. "I am not sure, it seems we will have to experiment. By the way, were you perhaps taking it easy on me when we went for a run yesterday?"

He laughed. "Yep, maybe just a little."

I just shook my head. "I thought so."

That's when I decided to get my revenge, and I pushed Damien down on the sofa and started to tickle him mercilessly.

Chapter Fourteen
Damien

Pat returned from putting his belongings away with a deeply perturbed expression on his face. "Who has been sleeping in my bed?"

I flinched and scratched my head. "Sorry, Pat, it was Brian and I, Papa Bear." Everyone snickered.

"Well, you could at least have made the bed."

I giggled. "We had planned to make it right after breakfast."

Matt interjected, "Do not be too hard on them, it was mostly my idea. Damien's bed was a little small for both of them."

Pat merely smirked. "It is alright, I am just busting their chops. Brian, I have talked with Mrs. Crabtree, and you will be accompanying Damien to therapy once a week to discuss everything that happened."

Brian looked over at me. "Thank you, Pat. I am just glad it is all out in the open now."

Pat grinned. "Today, we also have some work to do. I extended an invitation to Mrs. Crabtree and the rest of the foster kids from the house for a good old-fashioned barbecue. Damien and Brian, I need you to get the grill out of the barn and clean it up. Matt and I will go to the store and pick up the necessary provisions. Mrs. Crabtree will be preparing the salad and side dishes, and we will get to finally meet Mr. Crabtree—he's in town for Labor Day."

I was shocked. "Wow, I only saw him once the entire time I stayed there."

Matt leaned over and whispered, "Indeed, it appears even Mr. Crabtree now appreciates his wife's newfound demeanor. Nonetheless, it is still too bad that there are still a lot of individuals out there who believe the way she used to."

I sighed. "Now we have to go back to school and keep our relationship a secret. It will be a challenge not to be able to touch Brian or kiss him."

Brian grasped my hand firmly. "I know it is going to be difficult, but fortunately we do not have any classes together. Also, we have places to go where we can express ourselves."

Matt expressed, "I am confident that both of you will make some friends this year. Keep in mind that things are getting better and a lot will change after high school. The gay community no longer has to hide in the way we used to. How about a family group hug, what do you say?"

We all initially groaned and rolled our eyes at first, but soon we rose to our feet and embraced one another for a long moment.

Pat said, "Alright, we have a lot to do before our guests arrive, so chop chop."

Pat and Matt left for the store. While Brian and I proceeded to make Pat's bed to prevent getting yelled at again, followed by retrieving the grill, thoroughly cleaning, and rinsing it. Upon their return, Pat and Matt took charge of preparing everything. Shortly after, two vehicles pulled up in the driveway and Mr. and Mrs. Crabtree with the children piled out. Maggie, the young girl with pigtails, dashed towards me and wrapped her arms around my legs.

"Damien, I miss you so much. Are you coming back to the house now that Mrs. Crabtree is a lot nicer now?"

I stooped down and gave her a big warm embrace. "Sorry Maggie, I found a permanent home now. I hope one day you find a house of your own as well."

"Will you come by and see us?"

"Of course I will, and I will take you to school just like before."

"I'm so glad that you and Brian are friends. I think everyone needs at least one friend to share everything with."

I glanced towards Brian with a warm smile. "Yes, we should always have at least one special friend whom we can share everything with. Why don't you go over with the rest of the kids? We will be eating shortly."

I placed a kiss on her forehead before she joined everyone else. I looked across the yard at everyone coming together as a family, which brought a smile to my face. It was truly a splendid day.

And then I wondered: has my life truly taken a turn for the better, and are all these people really my family? Only time will tell, but for now, I must savor these moments for as long as it lasts.

The End.

Keeper of the Forsaken

Damien the Devil
Book 3

Prologue
Something in the Fog.

There was a chill in the air, accompanied by a thick fog drifting in from the Ohio River. The riverside was virtually deserted, as few individuals braved venturing out in the dense mist— no one with good intentions, anyway. A mysterious aura permeated the atmosphere, as if the mist was infused with electricity, illuminating the bridge and pathway and casting an eerie glow. The only individuals who typically ventured out were a handful of law enforcement officers who patrolled the area to ensure that no nefarious activity occurred, as criminals were more inclined to target individuals on evenings such as these.

However, there were always some young lovers who couldn't resist the temptation of finding a secluded spot away from the prying eyes of their parents—and here was one such couple now. Following dinner and a movie, John and his girlfriend Joann parked their car beside the serene river.

The young man eagerly anticipated how far he was going to get with his girlfriend that evening. Despite months of intimate encounters, it was during their most recent date that they advanced to a more physical level and were on the verge of going all the way. Unfortunately, their intimate moment was abruptly interrupted by Joann's parents, and John was sent home with a terrible case of blue balls. But tonight, no one was around to disturb them, and thus far, the evening unfolded precisely as John had planned. Following their arrival, they settled in, and John selected some romantic music on the radio. He kissed Joann while gently tracing his hand along her shoulder, skimming the outside of her sweater, and just barely touching her breast. Joann gently withdrew and grasped his hand—not to stop him but rather to assist him in finding the perfect location to explore as she giggled in response.

The car's windows became fogged up as the young couple was about to take things further, but the mechanics of the car hindered them—it being a sporty two-seater with a manual transmission. They decided to venture outside. John retrieved a blanket from the trunk and gently took Joann's hand as they strolled along the riverside path. John wrapped the blanket around his cherished girlfriend, embracing her closely to keep her warm. His letterman jacket from high school offered him ample protection for the time being. They strolled for a while, and while the fog had initially been faint, as they continued along the river, it thickened to the point where visibility was limited to just a couple of feet ahead. Eventually, they arrived at the park and discovered a secluded spot near a row of benches, illuminated by a streetlight.

Suddenly, John heard the faint sound of someone sobbing. He then turned to his girlfriend, asking, "Joann, do you hear that?"

Suddenly, John heard the faint sound of someone sobbing. He turned to his girlfriend and asked, "Do you hear that?"

"Yeah, it sounds like a young girl crying. I wish I could see better in this dense fog. John, perhaps we should consider going back?"

"But what if she's injured? We can't just abandon her here."

"Wasn't there a police officer further down the path near the car? We ought to let him investigate the situation."

"But we're right here, it'll only take a moment."

"John, you've taken me to enough scary movies for me to know that going off into the fog at night never turns out well."

John rolled his eyes. "That's just Hollywood for you."

The couple proceeded cautiously to investigate the area. The crying became more pronounced as they advanced, and eventually, they could make out a silhouette seated on a distant bench. As they got closer, it became apparent that the figure was a young girl, dressed in a formal party dress. She was about Joann's age and was hunched over in floods of tears.

Joann paused, while John advanced toward her and gently extended his hand to touch her shoulder. "Excuse me, are you alright? Do you require any assistance?"

Joann winced and trembled in response to the cold air, convinced that the temperature was dropping. "John, is she alright?"

John gestured for her to remain behind him as he turned and leaned over the girl. Suddenly, the girl looked up at John and let out a piercing scream directly in his face. Her visage was pale and white, her eyes as dark as the depths of night itself. Startled by this unforeseen outburst, John stumbled backward and landed before his girlfriend. Joann extended her hand to assist him to his feet. The weeping girl slowly rose and emitted one final scream at the couple before disappearing into the fog. John eventually regained his footing and took Joann's hand as they returned to their vehicle.

Joann was now crying and trembling herself. "What on earth was that?"

John's voice cracked as he uttered, "I'm not sure, but I think we need to get out of here."

They retraced their steps along the path, but the thick fog obscured their vision. Inadvertently, John collided with a trash can. Sensing they were nearing their vehicle, they suddenly encountered what looked like a silhouette of a man ahead. John speculated that the individual approaching could be the police officer responsible for nighttime patrols in the area. However, upon closer inspection, it became clear that this was a young guy wearing a high school letterman jacket similar to his own. With his back turned towards them, John reached for his shoulder, causing the man to turn around and face him. Just like the girl in the park, his face was all white, and his eyes were a deep black. The mysterious figure then parted his lips, allowing his jaw to drop, releasing a piercing scream that resonated in the night. Joann seized John's arm, and they bolted. Glancing back, John noticed the figure had vanished into the fog. Before long, they reached the car, where John fumbled with his keys, accidentally dropping them. After swiftly retrieving them, he unlocked the car door for Joann before circling around to enter on his side. John's hands trembled as he attempted to insert the keys into the ignition. As he started the car and prepared to shift into reverse, a beam of light illuminated him. John felt a wave of relief wash over him as he rolled down the window and saw a police officer.

"What are you youngsters doing outside at this hour? It isn't very safe out here in this dense fog."

John was out of breath but tried to regain his composure. "I know. We're just leaving. But I want you to know there is something really strange out there…"

"Alright, try to calm down and tell me what happened."

John and Joann did their best to recount what had happened to them to the officer. The officer asked them how much they'd had to drink tonight, but John assured him they hadn't had a drop. The officer had a grin on his face and appeared somewhat skeptical, but nonetheless, he took down their names and phone numbers before telling them to drive safely.

Chapter One: Damien
Need more time.

It's been nearly a year since Brian had his last nightmare. Regrettably, we have yet to identify the mysterious figure in the black cloak whom Brian encountered at the warehouse and recalled in his dreams. What do they want with me, and could it be related to my parents? Sometimes, I still feel like there is someone—or something—watching us. But whenever I bring up the subject to Pat and Matt, they skillfully change the subject. I understand they are just trying to keep me safe, but I wish somebody would just tell me what is going on—I'm no longer a child, after all.

Fortunately, now that I'm getting older, they let me help with some of their investigations, as long as it does not interfere with school. Pat has successfully got permission from Mr. Craft and Miss Crabtree for Brian to stay at the farmhouse with us until he has to leave for

Elsewhere, one of the islands located within the realm of Neverland. I understand he has no say in the matter, but I'm still struggling to deal with it.

Brian's last day is swiftly approaching. While the past few years have been truly wonderful, I wish we had more time to spend together—especially now that Brian and I have advanced our relationship following my sixteenth birthday. We're becoming increasingly intimate and find it difficult to resist the urge to touch each other. In fact, we eagerly engage in the exploration of each other's bodies whenever the opportunity arises. However, Brian has displayed great patience by refraining from pressuring me into situations I'm not ready for. We've not gone all the way. Based on what we have read in Matt's private collection of magazines when he is not home, I do not think I'm ready for that yet.

Nevertheless, we have discovered plenty to entertain ourselves with. The barn remains one of our favorite places to make out. Pat and Matt have become accustomed to knocking before entering, as they have unintentionally interrupted us in intimate moments before. Pat tends to steer clear of the topic entirely, whereas Matt is willing to answer any questions we may have—within reasonable limits, of course. However, he still becomes slightly nervous and tongue-tied when discussing what he refers to as "the bees and the bees."

We still have separate beds in my bedroom—primarily for keeping up appearances, because we're still too young to be shacking up with each other. But it's not like we can't sneak into each other's beds whenever we want to.

In our leisure time, when we're not studying for school, I occasionally assist Pat and Matt with a case now and then. Despite Pat's initial reluctance, I take great pleasure in visiting Mr. Craft at the office. Occasionally, I have the opportunity to talk to the new kids in the surrounding foster homes and help them get settled into their new homes—thus ensuring what happened to me doesn't happen to any other kids.

It was a challenging experience when I was placed in the Crabtree home—whoever thought putting a young gay vampeal under the care of someone with such a rigid, narrow-minded view of faith was a good idea? However, Miss Crabtree has found a new sense of direction in her life, thanks to a mysterious figure believed to be an elderly woman who frequents the park to feed the pigeons.

Unfortunately, there remains a significant number of individuals in the world who share the same narrow-minded views as she once did. I hope we see a future where children can freely develop their identities without fear of persecution, violence, and being abandoned and discarded like yesterday's trash. While there is a glimmer of hope for such a reality to exist one day, it's probable that there will always be a part of society that harbors animosity towards people different from themselves.

Chapter Two: Pat
Reunion

Mr. Craft requested that I stop by the Feral Society's office. Upon arrival, I went to the main office, where Miss Periwinkle was at her desk as usual. The office was still an understated room with old tile flooring and a shabby wooden desk that resembled a government agency lacking proper funding.

Miss Periwinkle, pleasant as always, smiled warmly. "Ah, Mr. Davison, right on schedule. Mr. Craft is expecting you, please go inside."

I expressed my gratitude to her and proceeded to enter Mr. Craft's proper office (this first office was a front to deter unwanted visitors, Mr. Craft was a short man with a face that resembled a bulldog. However, appearances can be deceiving—he could be a real teddy bear when you get to know him.

Mr. Craft got up from his desk and came around it, warmly welcoming me. "Mr. Davidson, I'm so happy to see you. How are Damien and Brian doing?"

I smiled in response. "They're great—still two love-sick kids that can't keep their hands off each other."

"How are they coping with Brian leaving soon?"

"They don't seem to be dwelling on it too much. I sincerely hope that it doesn't hit Damien too hard. You never forget your first love."

"Indeed. That's a topic we're all too familiar with. Anyway, allow me to get to the point of my summoning you here today. I believe this particular matter aligns perfectly with your expertise, Mr. Davidson. Reports have surfaced regarding ghosts roaming in the vicinity of both the river and the warehouse district."

"Mr. Craft, do you believe they're ghosts of children who fell victim to the vampire?"

"We do indeed believe this to be the case. It will have required a considerable amount of time for them to accumulate sufficient energy to manifest their presence. Furthermore, there've been ongoing renovations in the vicinity. Although we initially believed we had discovered all the remains from that tragic evening, and hoped they had all passed on, it's possible that we overlooked a few.

"The other evening, as the fog rolled in off of the river, a young couple, just as exuberant as your boys at home, was scared out of their wits by the sight of two ghosts. They informed a patrolling police officer of their encounter, prompting him to conduct a thorough investigation. Despite initially spotting the ghosts wandering amidst the warehouses, he eventually lost track of them. That's when they called for my assistance, recognizing our superior ability to manage such peculiar occurrences."

"That's fantastic. I'll certainly investigate further. It's unfortunate that my brother is currently away, since he could have been a real help."

"I know you make a great team. However, your boys will be available to help out, even though I understand you prefer to keep Damien away from this situation. Now they know his location, we can't keep him hidden forever. Over the past few years, he has become a resourceful young man. Besides, I have full confidence in your ability to confront a few spectral entities."

"I'm inclined to agree with you," I said. "Still, I'm worried about the intentions of the mysterious figure in the hood. I'm also convinced all these events are connected in some way."

"I share your apprehensions, which is why I have a little gift for you. Please come through."

Now I was intrigued by what the old man was up to. It had become apparent to me that he always had a hidden agenda. Still, despite his cunning nature, it was clear that his intentions were good. As we approached the bookcase, we carefully selected a volume by Edgar Allan Poe, revealing a secret passage leading to the inner sanctum of the real organization. The interior exuded a Victorian charm, illuminated by ornate brass sconces that adorned rich, dark wood and textured wallpaper.

Mr. Craft paused at the entrance to his real office. "I've arranged for someone to assist you. I believe you are well acquainted with his exceptional abilities."

Mr. Craft opened the door to the lavishly furnished room, to find a distinguished gentleman seated in one of the elegant, high-backed leather chairs. As the man rose to greet him, a smile involuntarily graced my lips upon recognizing the familiar face of my former college companion, Steven. I couldn't help but wonder about the nature of this unexpected visit from my ex-boyfriend.

"Mr. Davidson, I trust you're already acquainted with Mr. Miller. I've enlisted his expertise to assist you in delving into this case in your brother's absence. His unique talent for psychometry is bound to prove invaluable."

Mr. Craft's observation was indeed accurate. Steven possessed the unique ability to visualize images by physical contact. He had to consistently wear gloves to prevent accidentally triggering visions, as his ability wasn't something he could simply switch off at will. Despite this challenge, Steven pursued a degree in criminology and was currently serving as a detective in the Dayton police force. Very little escaped his keen observation, and I was fully aware of his full range of talents. As I extended my hand in a gesture of professionalism, Steven reciprocated with a warm smile. I must confess that Steven is the one person with whom I struggle to maintain a professional demeanor. Despite our separation, those old feelings bubble up when I'm with him, even though I haven't seen him in a few years.

Mr. Craft laughed. "There's no need to be so formal. I understand the depth of your relationship. Hug it out, and then we can proceed with our work."

After exchanging a warm embrace, we took a seat as Mr. Craft handed us a dossier detailing our tasks: investigating the eerie occurrences along the river, and aiding the unsettled spirits to find peace. We thanked Mr. Craft, and said goodbye to Miss Periwinkle on the way out.

I followed Steven next to his car. "I'm so pleased to see you. It's been quite a while. How have you been?"

"It's a pleasure to see you again, Patrick. I'm doing well—I'm mostly occupied with work cases, but I have the occasional night off now and then. Have you been romantically involved with anyone lately?"

"No, I'm currently single, and Mr. Craft has been keeping me busy with work. I've actually been caring for a child named Damien. He is a vampeal and largely well-behaved, but can be quite challenging at times. His partner is also living with us until he reaches the age of eighteen, after which he must return home to Neverland to avoid rapidly aging. I'll provide you with more details once we arrive at the house. Can you remember the way?"

"To your parents' farmhouse? It's been a while, but I think so. So, Damien's boyfriend is a Lost Boy? How intriguing!"

Chapter Three: Damien
The Guest.

    I replaced the receiver in the kitchen and once again found myself wishing that Pat and Matt would install an additional telephone line in the living room. This way, I wouldn't have to jump up and run into the kitchen each time the phone rang.

    The advantage of Brian staying at the house was that neither Pat nor Miss Crabtree would be yelling at us to get off the phone in case someone called. Still, isn't that normal behavior for teens in love? This leads us back to my first point: installing a secondary phone line would resolve the issue. It's not like they couldn't afford it. Matt and Pat get paid well, or so I understand. Fortunately, we do have cable TV since there's hardly any reception out here in the middle of nowhere. Brian and I spend most of our time watching music videos on MTV, enjoying the latest chart hits. We live approximately twenty minutes away from the foster home by car or, in Matt's case, by truck. It's remarkably quiet out here, so if we really want to do anything, we have to go back into town. Brian drives us to school because there isn't a school bus that comes this far out.

Upon entering the living room, I found Brian reclining comfortably on the couch. I nestled myself beside him.

"Damien, who was on the phone?"

"It was Pat, calling to let us know he's on his way home. He mentioned that a new case has come up and that he needs our help."

"That sounds interesting. Did he say anything about what it's about?"

"No, but he did mention that he has a surprise for me."

"Wow, I wonder what it could be…"

Shortly after, I heard Pat arrive in Matt's truck. Intrigued, I proceeded to the kitchen and peered through the window of our back door, only to notice a second vehicle trailing behind him. I caught sight of a tall, thin blond guy, roughly the same age as Pat, wearing jeans and a white shirt. The only thing that struck me as strange was that he wore black leather gloves. When I saw his face, it seemed familiar, evoking a sense of déjà vu, yet I struggled to recall where I'd seen him before.

I swiftly ran back and jumped on the couch next to Brian. Brian glanced over at me. "What's up, Damien?"

"Pat's brought someone with him. I'm not sure who he is… Pat's never brought anyone home before."

Pat and his guest entered through the kitchen door, calling out as they approached the living room. "Damien, Brian, I'm home and I have a guest. This is…"

Just as he was about to introduce me, I suddenly recollected where I had previously seen that face. Despite never having officially met him in person, I instantly recognized him. Without thinking, I blurted out, "It's Steven, your ex-boyfriend from college, correct? I remembered seeing his picture on your office desk."

Pat shot me his customary annoyed look. "Yes, this is Steven, otherwise known as Detective Miller. He'll be staying for a while, offering assistance on the case Mr. Craft assigned us."

My attention was piqued when he mentioned us. "Does that mean Brian and I get to help?"

"Yes, Damien. Mr. Craft thought that your involvement in this matter might be useful in this case because we have some unresolved business down by the warehouse. There've been reports of people seeing ghosts down by the park and the river. Although unconfirmed, it appears that some of the kids killed at the warehouse may not have found peace, and we need to investigate to see if we overlooked anything. There's also a chance we might find more information on the strange hooded figure that Brian encountered that night he was taken by the vampire."

"So why is Steven here? Sorry, I don't mean to be rude but what's with the gloves? It's not that cold out."

Steven stepped forward. "It's a pleasure to meet the both of you. I've heard a lot about you boys. Yes, Patrick and I were romantically involved during our college years, but now I'm a member of Mr. Craft's specialized law enforcement unit that deals with cases beyond the scope of regular police work. I can visualize images of things I touch, hence the gloves. It's called psychometry. While this ability certainly proves invaluable, it isn't infallible."

My eyes widened in astonishment. "Oh my goodness, that is amazing! It's such a shame that Matt is out of town; this would be right up his alley. I'm finally going to get the opportunity to see a real-life ghost! Well, so to speak. Pat, do you think we will be able to see them?"

"Woah, Damien, let's slow down a bit. The manifestation of these entities requires a significant amount of time and energy before they become visible to everyone. That may explain why it took so long for them to make their presence known. Also, they're doing some renovations near the warehouse, which may contribute to the current disturbance. We'll likely only catch fleeting glimpses of them before they disappear."

Brian grabbed my hand firmly and drew a deep breath before inquiring, "Pat, do you believe we missed finding some of the kids? Seeing the dead bodies wasn't very pretty last time."

"I'm not sure, but whoever the spirits are, it seems they have something they want us to know."

I heard rumbling from my stomach. "When do you plan on starting? I hope we can get something to eat soon. I'm starving."

Pat laughed. "Ah, the insatiable appetites of my boys, always thinking about their stomachs. However, we should get started tonight after dark. The local authorities are aware of our investigation. Still, I can't in good conscience let you go out on an empty stomach. So what are you boys hungry for?"

As if Pat needed to ask. "What do you think about pizza with all the fixings?"

Pat smiled and turned towards Steven. "Does that meet with your approval?"

"Sure, Pat. It'll be just like old times."

"Very well, it's decided then—the usual for everyone."

Chapter Four: Pat
Ghost Hunting.

I wonder if it was such a good idea stuffing the boys with all that pizza. I could never see where exactly they managed to store it all. They consumed an entire pizza by themselves. Still, I remember our parents expressing similar sentiments when Matt and I were growing up.

In preparation, I assembled all the necessary equipment for the evening: flashlights, a thermometer for monitoring temperature fluctuations, and an EMF meter for detecting electrical currents. While I could bring a camera, I wasn't really interested in capturing images and proving the existence of ghosts and spirits to the world. We simply need to locate their remains, provide them with a proper burial, and allow them to move on.

We all grabbed our jackets and climbed into Matt's truck. Steven and I took the front seats, while Damien and Brian settled in the back. Upon arrival, we noticed that the authorities had cordoned off the section of the river where the apparitions were said to have been sighted, allowing us to conduct our investigation. The air was damp, as though it had just rained. I provided the boys with the necessary equipment to measure fluctuations in temperature or electrical current. Damien was excited to see his first ghost after Matt and I shared our experiences over the years. I must confess that I felt a sense of joy at the prospect of working with Steven. Several years had passed since his departure to pursue bigger and better opportunities in New York, but it seemed to have overwhelmed him, prompting his return to the suburbs of Dayton.

Walking down the pathway, we came across a lamppost that guided our way along the river. A few of them began to intermittently flicker, and as we approached, we saw the silhouette of a young man wearing a letterman jacket, hunched over near a bench. He appeared to have paused to regain his composure, prompting me to approach him. He was breathing heavily and muttering something to himself that I couldn't make out. As I approached him, I noticed a sudden drop in temperature, causing my breath to become visible in the night air. I reached out to touch his shoulder, but when he turned, his complexion was very pale, almost white, his eyes hollow and dark. A look of sheer terror was etched on his face. He let out a piercing scream, raising his arms in a defensive gesture against something that we couldn't see. Then, he abruptly turned and ran off toward the river, disappearing into the darkness of the night.

I turned towards Steven, who proceeded to remove his gloves and began to work investigating the surroundings. Damien and Brian stood there in awe, their mouths gaping wide open. As usual, I had to go over and close them, plus I was curious to check for any data on the equipment.

Damien began darting about like a playful puppy chasing its tail. "Pat, oh my goodness, was that a ghost? Is that what you and Matt see all the time?"

"I rarely get to see ghosts—that particular phenomenon is more in line with my brother's expertise, unless the spirit in question specifically wishes to reveal itself to me. I have my suspicions regarding the nature of this haunting. Let Steven conclude his investigation here before we proceed to the next location."

Shortly thereafter, Steven put his gloves back on and came over to share his findings. "This is the location where the young man was assaulted; however, I do not believe he was killed at this site—the spirit of the victim does not linger here. I'm only perceiving residual images from this one event."

It was as anticipated, yet Damien and Brian both appeared somewhat confused.

"Gentlemen, did your instruments get any readings?" Steven asked.

Damien glanced over at Brian, who smiled and scratched his head. "Sorry, I guess in all the excitement we forgot to look. So Pat, was that a ghost or not?"

I smiled reassuringly. "Don't worry, I understand you didn't know what to expect. It was your first time, but from now on, keep one eye on the readings. They are crucial, especially when we get closer to finding them. This phenomenon is known as a residual haunting. It's like a playback from an incident captured on video of a traumatic event. However, it's not the source of the problem. I believe we will encounter a similar scenario at the other site within the park. It's clear the victims weren't killed at this location—rather, they were likely taken elsewhere, possibly in the vicinity of the warehouse. Let's hope we uncover more information at the next site."

As we proceeded further along the path, memories of the night that Damien was kicked out of the foster home flooded my mind. Despite always putting on a brave face, he must have been scared. It's only natural for anyone in his circumstances. Now nearly two years later and here we are, back in the same place and still trying to make sense of it all. Damien was nearing his seventeenth birthday, and Brian was due to turn eighteen in a few days—which meant he needed to return to Neverland, or he would start aging at an accelerated rate.

As we approached the park, I felt a sense of unease creep over me, causing the hairs on the back of my neck to stand on end. I could hear the sounds of a girl crying in the distance. The lights started to flicker again, accompanied by a sudden temperature drop once more. Glancing at the boys beside me, I quietly informed them that we were getting close. They nodded in unison and glanced at their instruments, signaling to me with a thumbs up that they were successfully getting a reading.

The sound of sobbing kept getting louder, then I saw a young lady seated on a bench, crying with her head resting in her hands. We all surrounded the bench, yet she never stopped crying—she seemed oblivious to our presence. She was wearing a light blue dress, with one of the sleeves appearing torn. The damage didn't look like the handiwork of a vampire. I approached her, but she met my gaze with a look of horror, her face drained of all color and her eyes sunken in, just like the young man's. She raised her arms in a defensive gesture, as though fending off an unseen attacker, then stumbled to the ground, before rising and fleeing in the opposite direction, passing right through Steven. He jerked to the side as if he was being pushed out of the way, then she vanished as well.

Brian assisted Steven to a nearby bench, where Damien and I joined them. I extended my hand towards Steven in a gesture of support.

I turned to Damien and asked, "Did you get a response?"

"Oh yeah! There was a noticeable increase in the meter. I don't know why I didn't realize it before. I can sense her energy easily and don't need the instruments to tell me that. It was remarkably strong, but it's slowly returning to normal now. That was such a trip!"

Steven once again went through his customary routine, removing his gloves and carefully examining the bench. Steven's expression seemed sad as he made his way back towards us.

"So what did you discover?"

"Poor girl was deeply emotional, and it's the same as the other occurrence—an echo of the event. Initially, she had a dispute with her boyfriend. He became somewhat aggressive while tearing her dress, and when she forced him to stop, he walked away. The young man likely fell victim to an initial assault before the vampire pursued her, attacking her just over there, right before ultimately abducting her to conceal the evidence."

I placed my hand gently on Steven's shoulder; I knew how hard it was for him to see pictures in his mind of such violence. "How are you holding up?"

"Just give me a moment. Unfortunately it's not the first time, and we both know it likely won't be the last. I'm just surprised how the boys are handling the situation. It couldn't have been easy for either of them."

"They've been resolving their issues with the assistance of their therapist. Honestly, I've come to admire the resilience and fortitude displayed by both of them."

Steven embraced me warmly before we both redirected our attention towards the boys. "Shall we proceed?"

The warehouse was to be our next destination.

Chapter Five: Damien
Back to where it all began.

As we made our way to the warehouse, I realized how overwhelmed I was with everything going on this evening. I got to see real ghosts—or what Pat referred to as spectral remnants of them—which was a phenomenon entirely new to me. It hasn't been easy coaxing Pat and Matt to open up about their work.

I vividly recall everything about the night I was kicked out of the house, encountering the red-haired vampire. I grasped for Brian's hand—I'm aware that was a painful experience for him as well, as the night turned into a battle for our very survival. I don't know how I managed it. I didn't have the opportunity to think about what to do. I simply did what I had to. Whether I was driven by instinct or reflex, I really didn't know.

Now that we'd returned to the place where it all began, when we got to the warehouse, I noticed that certain structures had been demolished and others were undergoing renovations. Surprisingly, the warehouse where I spent the night when I was kicked out still remained untouched. We made our way through some of the heavy machinery and mounds of dirt, finally reaching the staircase leading to the back door of the basement. As I grabbed the doorknob, I realized that after all this time they had managed to repair the locks on the door. It's such a shame that I had to resort to breaking it once more.

As I began to turn the handle, Pat intercepted me and flashed a smile while presenting the keys. He informed me, "Mr. Craft managed to contact the owner and secure the keys for us, to prevent any further damage to the door."

I asked Pat, "So, who does the warehouse belong to?"

"A wealthy gentleman, Mr. James, the owner of a chain of import-export furniture establishments known as Magnolia Emporium. He was particularly keen that his identity wasn't disclosed to the press when we discovered the deceased teenagers. There should be electricity down here."

Pat unlocked the door, and we entered the room, reaching for the light switch along the wall. With a flick of the switch, the single light bulb in the room suddenly flashed and then went out a moment later. We pulled out some flashlights and a battery-operated lantern, and positioned them on a table that was still covered in a sheet—just like it was the night I slept there. I approached the sofa where I discovered Brian passed out. There were still some traces of dried blood staining it. Brian grasped my hand tightly, and I saw the anguish on his face. I put my other arm around him, trying to comfort him. Together we both took a deep breath and released it in unison.

Brian informed Steven that he was seated on this couch, while the other bodies occupied the one to the right. Steven examined the sofa where Brian had been seated, before moving on to the other one. As he ran his bare hands over the fabric, his expression grew increasingly focused. Occasionally, he would wince as if he were in pain. His breathing became more pronounced as he shifted towards the opposite side. Afterwards, he then moved to other pieces of furniture. I wonder what thoughts and emotions ran through his mind as he moved around the room. He still had the same intense look on his face. Once Steven was done, he put his gloves back on and settled into a chair, his expression blank. Pat knelt beside Steven, grasping his hand, revealing a side of his character I'd never seen before.

After Steven regained his composure, he told us what information he had uncovered. "I must commend your bravery in facing the ordeal you experienced. The vampire who assaulted you wasn't simply upset about the events of that night—his animosity runs much deeper than that. The ghosts we are looking for aren't here, but those unfortunate souls he killed were. He didn't just kill them, he tortured and fed off of them for a long time. The lingering memory of their deaths continues to stain this place, and probably will for a long time. However, they have now found peace and have passed on. The fate of the other couple appears to be unrelated. We're going to have to keep looking."

Suddenly, I got the feeling that we weren't alone. I scanned the room, noticing a shadow in the corner move slightly. I pointed the flashlight at the corner, and there was someone dressed in a black hooded cloak, just as Brian described. Rising to my feet, I alerted the others that there was someone in the room with us. Despite Pat's warning, I advanced towards the mysterious figure. However, as I moved closer, the hooded man vanished without a trace, melding seamlessly into the darkness.

"Damien, please stop! Let him go, we don't know what we're up against yet. You haven't had the opportunity to feed, meaning you're at a disadvantage right now. I don't believe that he was planning to do us any harm, or he would have done it before now. Let's call it a night and regroup in the morning, when it'll be safer. Steven, have you learned anything from our mysterious friend?"

"No, I couldn't capture clear details of the hooded individual, only obtaining blurred images. It appears that its presence was brief, although the vampire seemed to exhibit a combination of anger and fear towards this mysterious hooded figure."

Pat rose to his feet and folded his arms across his chest. "I would rather not take any chances with you boys getting hurt again, so let's gather our belongings and get out of here. We can pick up where we left off tomorrow morning."

But I was so excited and eager to learn more while we were here. Although I could have voiced my objections, I realized there was no point—Pat was probably right, as usual.

As we retraced our steps to the truck, Steven informed the other officers that we were done for the night.

Upon returning to the house, we carelessly tossed everything on the couch, feeling a mix of exhaustion and exhilaration from what we learned tonight. Brian and I retired to our room, while Pat and Steven stayed in Pat's bedroom downstairs. With all the excitement, I wondered if any of us would manage to get any sleep tonight.

Chapter Six: Damien.
Did someone get lucky?

I was able to catch some sleep, even though I was still wound up from last night. I woke Brian by giving him a gentle kiss on the forehead. He grabbed me, pulling me back onto the bed. I playfully tickled his side, causing him to squirm and wriggle beneath me. His laughter filled the air as he begged me to stop. He was getting taller and his body was filling out, but he still was no match for me. I persisted as tears started to run down his face, only stopping as I got a whiff of something delightful coming from the kitchen.

Brian was lucky that my stomach saved him.

"Hey, do you smell that?"

"Oh yeah, someone is baking a batch of biscuits."

Both of us took turns attending to our morning routines, then threw on pajama bottoms before making our way downstairs. I was more than a little surprised to discover Pat and Steven cooking in the kitchen together. They stood there, bare-chested and in pajama bottoms, and they were both laughing and carrying on like a young couple. I don't think I'd ever seen Pat without a shirt on, as opposed to Matt who frequently lost his shirt all the time because he liked working out. Steven, on the other hand, still had his gloves on, and I wondered if he always wore them. Also, I noticed that Pat appeared way more relaxed.

I turned towards Brian and gently nudged him. "Do you think they… did it last night?"

Brian chuckled. "He does seem happy. Imagine if your sexy ex-boyfriend came into town and he spent the night… What would you do?"

I just scratched my head and smiled. "Well, I know what I would do."

I never considered the idea of Pat doing it with anyone—but when it came to Matt, it was a different story. I wondered about the possibility of them getting back together, and Steven moving in—what if they started kissing? That would be so weird.

Brian nudged me because he sensed I was starting to overthink the whole thing. Everything smelled so wonderful, and it was making my mouth water. My stomach growled, and I was getting really hungry. A sumptuous feast had been prepared, the whole works—the menu included eggs, bacon, toast, biscuits, and hash browns.

Pat turned around and smiled. "Please go ahead and dig in, boys—there's plenty for everyone. You'll need your strength today."

Growing up in foster homes most of my life, I've learned to appreciate such moments. Brian and I seated ourselves at the table and filled our plates. Pat remained standing there smiling as we stuffed our faces, his coffee in his hand as usual. I noticed that he rarely joined us at the table to eat—instead, he was happy simply watching us.

"Aren't you both going to sit down and eat?" I asked him and Steven.

Steven was standing close to Pat, and I noticed a slight blush on Pat's cheeks. "We're fine, Damien. We were picking all morning while we were preparing breakfast."

I found myself unable to resist the urge. I felt I had to get more information from these two. It seemed easier to just blurt it out than to beat around the bush. "Do you think Matt will be pleased that you got lucky last night, and does Steven wear the gloves while in the bedroom?"

Pat choked and nearly spat out his coffee, while Steven turned and looked the other way. Brian just giggled. That was quite the challenge with a mouth full of food.

"Damien, not that it's any of your business what I do behind closed doors, but I'm pretty sure Matt's aware of the situation—it's a twin thing. We just seem to have a bond that allows us to sense each other's thoughts and emotions. Sometimes I wish I really didn't know what my brother was doing."

"I take that as a yes, then?"

Pat gave me his signature glance, indicating that was enough.

"Young man, you don't need to know what I do in private, just like I don't need to know what you both get up to in the barn."

"That's fair enough, I guess," I said with a smile.

Pat told us to finish up and get dressed so we could continue our investigation.

**Chapter Seven: Pat
Unearthed.**

Steven and I loaded the boys into the truck as we made our way back to the warehouse. It was a few minutes before noon, which ensured we'd have ample daylight to proceed with our investigation. I'm not sure who or what was lurking in the shadows last night, but I wasn't prepared to have a confrontation with it until I had more information about what we were up against.

Still, I strongly suspected it was a creature of the night—maybe an upper-level vampire or demon. It seemed to be observing, focusing particularly on Damien, with the rest of us just along for the ride. It all goes back to Damien and his parents. Why did they conceal him for so long, and why was there a veil of silence surrounding his being a vampeal?

When we arrived at the construction site, we surveyed our surroundings. I was mindful of keeping the boys within our sights, not allowing them to stray too far. Steven also arranged for additional support outside the premises if necessary. Despite these precautions, I knew I couldn't shield them from every potential danger as they grew older. It had become clear that I needed to place my trust in their ability to handle themselves.

I had hoped that the police dogs would have discovered something more substantial when they took the bodies from the warehouse, but the trail had now gone cold. That incident occurred two years ago, and it wasn't until last year that Brian began to experience his recurring dreams. The boys were growing up fast, and I was doing my best to shield them from all this crazy stuff, at least until they completed their schooling. Although they were still children, they were growing up so fast—falling in love, eventually leaving home, and that's the way it should be. Damien was welcome to stay as long as he wanted; I've grown fond of the mischievous monster. However, I knew I couldn't stop him from doing whatever his heart desires.

The site was filled with heavy machinery and mounds of dirt and gravel. Fortunately, they hadn't started laying the foundations and were still digging the area to install the plumbing and electricity. Considering this site spanned the size of a football field, the task at hand seemed like searching for a needle in a haystack. To simplify matters, Damien needed an energy boost. I was confident that Brian and I would be sufficient; however, Steven insisted on joining us.

Damien and I interlocked hands with Steven and Brian, forming the links of the chain. We all recoiled, holding onto one another as it only took a few seconds for the swift transference of energy to Damien. With the transfer of power emanating from each of us, the drain became less strenuous, and recovery only took a few minutes.

Afterwards, Steven and I took our position at the front, even though we knew Damien was still our best defense in case something unforeseen happened. It slipped my mind that when Damien siphoned life energy from someone with special talents, he acquired those same gifts temporarily. He would likely see visions when he came into contact with objects—inherited from Steven—and would hear spirits just like I did. It was quite amusing when Damien jumped back in surprise upon touching an object, triggering his first vision. Steven instructed him to touch things lightly with his fingertips, just to get the slightest of impressions. However, I could still see how his expression changed when he touched various objects.

After approximately an hour of looking around and not turning up anything substantial, the wind began to pick up, and rain started to fall. Realizing that we were too far from the truck and the warehouse, we sought refuge in a trailer at the far end of the construction site. Despite finding the door locked, Damien twisted the handle, allowing us to enter just as the rain started. Steven put his gloves back on and advised Damien he shouldn't touch anything. Brian and Damien sat by an old wooden desk, where I observed a portable transistor radio placed nearby.

"Hey Brian, would you mind checking the radio for a weather update?"

"Certainly, let's see if these batteries still work."

Brian retrieved the black radio with silver knobs, extending the antenna before flicking the switch to power it on. Slowly turning the dial to find a station, the announcer forecasted intermittent showers for the next hour before the imminent arrival of intense thunderstorms. Furthermore, all surrounding counties would be under a tornado warning till eight p.m. tonight.

When the rain momentarily subsided, I thought we should leave before it started again. I didn't want us to be in a trailer if a tornado hit.

"Okay guys, let's turn everything off and leave everything as we found it."

We started to leave when Damien grabbed my arm. "Pat, look over there, in that ditch by the trees. What is that?"

I caught a glimpse of something, but it was too small to make out from this distance. We hurried over to what Damien discovered. The trench had recently been excavated by the bulldozers, and there were two things protruding from the dirt. It appeared to be a sleeve from someone's varsity jacket, plus a girl's shoe. I instructed the boys to search the vicinity for a shovel. The winds had subsided, and I looked upwards—the sky appeared clear at the moment. However, I could see some dark clouds looming in the distance, hinting at an impending storm. If we were lucky, we had approximately thirty minutes before the storm hit.

Brian and Damien stumbled upon a pair of shovels leaning against the trailer, and they jumped in the ditch with them. With determination, they dug out the side where the jacket had been found, pulling it out. As they delved deeper, they uncovered the shoe. As they tossed both objects up to us, a leather wallet slipped out of one of the jacket's pockets. Despite their efforts, the boys could not uncover any further items during their search.

Looking up at the sky, I knew that time was running out. "Damien, Brian, that'll suffice for now. We must leave before the storm hits. We'll examine what we found later, and return tomorrow if necessary."

They agreed, and we hurried toward the truck. As we drove back home, the sky grew darker with each passing minute. Turning on the radio, we heard the announcer reporting a tornado that had touched down just a mile away.

Upon reaching our driveway, the rain began to fall once more. Seeking refuge, we made our way to the root cellar adjacent to the house. After opening the door, we all ducked inside as the wind picked up and the rain hammered down relentlessly. Securing the door as the wind whistled outside, we might as well make ourselves comfortable—it looked like we were going to be stuck in here until the storm passed.

Chapter Eight: Damien.
Weathering out the storm.

As Pat secured the door, the rest of us sought refuge in the root cellar just in time before the heavens opened. The wind picked up considerably, triggering a memory of an old movie that Pat and Matt liked so much, with a mysterious old crone on a bicycle and a young girl whisked away to a realm known as Oz. Oh crap! I just realized, if Neverland exists, could there possibly be an Oz as well? I wonder if Pat knows, or perhaps the crafty old Mr. Craft.

Thankfully, we were smart enough not to seek refuge in the house like the young girl in the movie. The one thing about Pat is his meticulous approach to planning ahead. By contrast, I tend to resemble Matt, often diving into situations guided by instinct. The cellar was well-stocked with provisions that Pat thought we might need. There was power for lighting and other essentials that Steven switched on when we entered. There was an ample supply of food, enough to sustain everyone for several days. There was a table and a whole bunch of folding chairs lining the walls, accompanied by a musty old cot and a pile of sleeping bags nestled in the far corner.

Steven switched on the radio to receive updates on the storm. Reports indicated that two tornadoes had now touched down, and the warning remained in effect until eight p.m., with the possibility of further developments. It seemed we were all stuck here until the radio announcer gave the all-clear.

He brought the jacket and the shoes, and placed them on the table. "Damien, I notice that when you absorb someone's energy, you occasionally tap into their innate talent."

"Yeah, it's occurred on several occasions."

"Then come over here, take a seat beside me, and place your hand on the jacket. Please share with us the images you see."

I closed my eyes and visualized the scene in my mind. "The red-haired vampire forced them back to the warehouse, but they resisted him every step of the way. He had not yet killed them for some reason, and had no intention of bringing them to the warehouse basement like he'd done with the other children. The boy wriggled out of his jacket and ran into the woods. The girl also attempted to flee, but in the process, she twisted her ankle, resulting in the loss of her shoe. Afterwards, the vampire knocked her out and dragged her some distance before abandoning her. He then pursued her boyfriend, disappearing into the woods. That's all I can see."

Steven grinned. "Well done, Damien. I arrived at a similar conclusion."

I observed the wallet and noted that this pair weren't runaways like the other kids in the basement. These two were high school students in the middle of a spat. I wonder whether someone had reported them as missing.

I turned to Pat and Steven. "They must be in the wooded area beyond the construction site. We should revisit there tonight following the storm to investigate what's out there."

Pat shook his head, and I could already anticipate his response. "No Damien, it's still too dangerous. I'll contact Mr. Craft to tell him of our findings and see if he knows anything more that could aid us. We're well aware who did this, and you know he isn't going anywhere—you killed him."

I acknowledged that I wouldn't win the argument, so I just agreed for the time being. The wind alternated between gusts and lulls, causing the door to shake now and then. Being down here was getting a little tiresome, and Brian and I found ourselves growing increasingly bored and hungry. Pat, anticipating our needs as ever, got out the snacks from the provisions that he had stored.

Everything appeared to be in order until a resounding thud echoed at the entrance of the underground storage. Startled, we all stumbled backward. Pat hurried to the door and pushed on it, but it wouldn't budge. It seems that something was wedged up against the door.

Offering to give it a try, I pushed with all my might, managing to shift it slightly, yet it was still firmly stuck. I tried again but this time Pat joined in. Despite our combined strength, it still wasn't enough. Brian asked if there were any tools to pry open the door, or dig our way out. Pat shook his head in disappointment. It seemed Pat's meticulous planning had encountered an unforeseen obstacle.

Steven had a funny expression on his face, indicating a state of deep contemplation.

"What if we all give Damien another power boost? But not a diluted one like before."

I pondered the idea that if a vampire could dig through six feet of dirt, then surely I should be able to get us out of here. Therefore, we all agreed, and one by one, they gave me their energy. The surge was nothing short of remarkable, instilling in me an unshakable belief in my abilities. I figured I should get a running start, so I propelled myself towards the door with all my might, hitting it hard. Upon impact, the door exploded and what was blocking the door went flying and landed right in front of Pat's truck, narrowly missing it. I winced as I turned to look at everyone as they came out of the cellar, knowing that I may have overdone it a bit.

Pat stood in awe, his gaze scanning the surroundings in disbelief. "All right, Superboy, you're going to fix the door tomorrow."

It was hard for them to see because the sun had already set, and there was a power outage. Pat proceeded to the generator next to the house and started it. However, I had no difficulty seeing in the darkness. The storm's aftermath had littered our surroundings with debris and various objects. The obstacle obstructing the door was a large old ice box, like the one at the nearby gas station.

When the lights came on in the house and the barn, everything appeared undamaged from my vantage point. I went over to the barn to get something to cover the door of the root cellar, but it became clear that there was nothing we could do that night.

It was after eight o'clock, and the radio announcer had given us the all-clear, so we got our stuff and returned to the house.

Chapter Nine: Damien.
Just couldn't stay home

We all gathered in the kitchen, as Pat's snacks in the root cellar really weren't cutting it. With no desire to cook, I assembled some sandwiches using lunch meat, bread, and various toppings. Brian grabbed some sodas and macaroni salad that Pat had prepared yesterday.

Upon trying the phone, Pat discovered it was dead, just like the electricity. Anticipating such situations, Pat and Matt had installed a gas generator a long time ago, given the frequent power outages out here in the sticks. We carried our feast into the living room and switched on the television to check for updates on any of the news channels. The power was out across the state, but fortunately, most of the urban areas were unscathed. However, some farmers and rural homes hadn't fared as well.

I turned to Pat and asked, "So what's the plan? Are we just going to sit here?"

"Damien, both of you will stay here. Steven and I are going out to the truck and getting on the CB radio to see if our assistance is required."

"Pat, we can help too?"

"No, you'll have to wait until tomorrow. This isn't open to discussion. I'm confident that you can occupy yourselves in the meantime…"

I rolled my eyes, but I knew that arguing was futile. Reluctantly I agreed, but as usual, I was formulating an alternative plan for when they left. Pat and Steven headed out the door and made their way to the truck, and talked for a bit before starting the engine. They turned on the headlights, including the spotlight on top, illuminating their surroundings as they turned around and sped out of the gravel driveway.

Returning to the living room, we settled onto the couch, and I started thinking.

Brian said, "I know I'm going to regret asking this, but what do you propose we do next? It's clear that you're planning something."

"Well, I can't just stay here and do nothing. After the boost you all gave me, I'm brimming with excess energy. We can't follow them because they'd spot us. I propose that we return to the construction site and start looking around the woods for the kids."

Brian sighed. "The last time we went out at night looking for something, it didn't work out so well."

"I know, but we weren't together then and are better equipped to handle ourselves now. I think there's something that can help. I'll be right back."

I ran up the stairs to Matt's room, grabbed an old brown leather case, then headed back downstairs to the living room, placing it on the dining room table.

"Damien, isn't that Matt's porn collection? How could that possibly help?"

"No, silly, that's in the other leather case. This is Matt's vampire hunter kit."

"Remarkable!"

I laid out an assortment of wooden stakes and metal ones as well, plus other objects, and explained the situation to Brian.

"These stakes are crafted from silver and would be lethal to a vampire if it were to penetrate its heart. However, silver has a dual purpose beyond killing a vampire, unlike in the case of werewolves. The chains and the silver dust are utilized to restrain the fiends, as the silver's burning effect means they can't free themselves if captured. Additionally, they could try to grab the wooden stakes, but they can't touch the silver ones. The same principle applies to crosses, and of course, the timeless classic, holy water. There's also a box of silver bullets here, but the guns are securely locked away in a cabinet in Pat's office."

"Damien, did you know that one of the components in pixie dust is silver? While many of the elements can be replicated, there are two ingredients that are hard to get—one remains a closely guarded secret, while the others are made from the ashes of pixies themselves. That's why there's not a lot of it around. However, the question remains—how are we supposed to get there? Pat left with the truck, and it isn't safe to take my car…"

I arched an eyebrow at Brian. "I believe you've already got that covered."

"What, in the darkness? The power is out all over the state, and you've never done a night flight. I can't risk you colliding with a tree again."

"I only did that once, and you were distracting me. If we get high enough, we should be able to see for miles, and there isn't a single cloud in the sky now that the storm's subsided. We can rely on the stars until we reach the vicinity of the city, where they still have power."

"Frankly, I'd rather be making out in the barn with you like Pat suggested. Still, I suppose I'm in. Someone has to keep you out of trouble."

We gathered all the necessary items before stepping outside. As I gazed up at the clear night sky, the stars shone brightly, and you would have never known the devastation the storm had wrought just a few hours ago. Brian extracted a pinch of enchanted dust from the leather pouch, and gently sprinkled it over both of us. Taking Brian's hand, I planted a kiss on his cheek as we ascended gracefully into the air, rising above the barn and the surrounding trees until we were hundreds of feet in the air.

Surveying the scene below, I noticed the gas station a few blocks away, its gas tanks having exploded and caught on fire. There were several fire trucks trying to extinguish the raging inferno. The tornado had passed dangerously close to us, as evidently that was the gas station's icebox in our driveway. Scanning the landscape, it was clear that the power outage extended for miles in every direction, except I could see that there was still power in the city down by the river. I could recognize the location where the park should be.

I gestured in the direction we needed to head, and Brian acknowledged my signal with a nod. I smiled, and we flew towards the park and the warehouse. I tightly held his hand as we gracefully maneuvered our way through the open skies.

Chapter Ten: Damien.
This Old House.

Soaring through the skies with Brian was an exhilarating experience. As we intertwined our fingers and ascended towards the clouds, then swiftly descended and elegantly maneuvered left and right, it felt like being on a rollercoaster, yet without the confines of the metal car. We were free to chart our course wherever we desired, guided only by the winds that wrapped around us effortlessly. The air has currents like the ocean, steering you wherever you need to go.

I've never had the opportunity to fly at night before, unlike Brian, who has soared through the night sky countless times, being one of the Lost Boys. It strikes me as funny that I'm yet to set foot inside an airplane, but have already flown through the sky. Peering down below, I noticed we were getting closer to the city. I never realized how beautiful the lights are from up here before.

One of the most cherished moments I shared with Brian was finding ourselves floating, suspended in the air with the ground far below us, holding each other while sharing a kiss. However, I'm aware all this won't last forever because Brian said it gets harder to fly when you grow up—something about all the stress and pressure of being an adult. They stop believing in the enchantment of their own imagination, causing the pixie dust to lose its efficacy. Not to mention that Brian will be leaving soon, and thus my supplier of pixie dust will be gone.

    I noticed the lights of the park coming up below. With no one in sight, we made a gentle landing. It took a lot of practice and time over the last few months to master the art of landing softly, but I think I'd perfected it by now. We proceeded to the bench where we had previously seen the young girl and though she wasn't visible, I still could hear her faint sobbing. Experiencing Pat's situation firsthand was a strange sensation, being able to hear something that can't be seen. Brian and I walked farther toward the warehouse and saw that it was still deserted. Eventually, we stumbled upon the trailer. Equipped with our flashlights, we noticed a path leading into the woods beyond the construction site.

    We were uncertain exactly where it went, but decided to follow it anyway. I was unfamiliar with this part of town, and so was unaware of what lay ahead—I just had a feeling. There was no need to call out because we knew the couple we were looking for weren't alive anymore, and probably wouldn't answer. I tried to focus my attention and listen to what was out there. It was strange, there was only silence—no chirping crickets or rustling creatures disrupted the quiet.

It was like the area was lifeless, giving me an unsettling feeling. I couldn't see any lights in the direction we were heading towards.

Just then, I suddenly heard the faint sounds of a girl crying once more.

I informed Brian I could hear her, and the sound seemed to be coming from a point further ahead. He followed closely behind me. Gradually, the cries grew louder until we reached a clearing that opened up to an ancient two-story manor house that appeared to have been partially consumed by fire on one side. From what I could see, the entire right wing of the house was pretty much gone, leaving behind only a charred skeleton of the once-grand estate. It was an eerie sight, especially with the moon casting a sinister glow over the surroundings. If this were a horror film, this would be the moment when the unsuspecting victims ought to heed the warning signs and turn back before it's too late.

A partially paved driveway led to the side of the house, while the rest of the yard was engulfed by overgrown weeds and grass, with the remnants of a broken picket fence that was probably painted white in its prime. An old dirt road led back into the woods from where we had come.

As we approached the entrance of the house, where a door should have stood, we were met with the sight of its rusted hinges and the door itself lying on a dirty wooden floor.

As we went inside, Brian grabbed my arm. "Perhaps this might not be a good idea. This house is falling apart. Maybe we should come back with Pat and Steven tomorrow morning."

"You're probably right, but now that we're here, I want to see where the crying is coming from. Once we find that out, then we can go back and tell Pat and Steven what we found. Let me see what's inside, and when I give you a signal, you follow right behind me."

"All right, but I don't like this."

I cautiously entered the foyer, and the wood timber groaned beneath the weight of my steps. Nature had taken over this old forsaken house, with dirt and heaps of leaves scattered about. A staircase led up to the second floor with only the left side still standing, while the right lay in ruins. The moonlight filtered through the remnants of the roof, casting a ghostly glow. I ran my fingers along the handrail of the aged stairs, feeling the thick residue of ash left by a long-forgotten fire. I got a mental picture of the couple being dragged across the floor towards a door situated at the rear of the room. I informed Brian that they were taken through a door out the back.

I cautiously started to make my way toward the door, mindful of the loud creaking of the floorboards beneath me. With great care, I navigated along the edge until I safely reached the door. I opened it and it gave way, falling to the floor with a deafening crash. I turned once more to inform Brian that I successfully made it, only to realize that he had already started to follow behind me. Just then, I noticed that he had reached the precise location where the floor was cracking, and before I had the opportunity to warn him, the floor beneath his feet suddenly collapsed, causing him to plummet through a hole in the floor.

I hurried to the opening and called out, "Brian, are you alright?"

Brian groaned as he brushed off the dust and attempted to rise to his feet, only to stumble and fall back. "I'm alright, but I think I may have twisted my ankle—it's hard to walk."

"Can you see anything down there?"

Brian retrieved his flashlight and surveyed his surroundings. "Yeah, I think I found the basement."

"Wait there, and I'll see if I can find the stairs."

Just as I located the door that led down to the basement, I heard the sound of a vehicle pulling up. Its headlights lit up the windows and the entrance of the old house. Gesturing to Brian to be quiet, I noticed two shadowy figures standing in the doorway. I couldn't make out who they were, since they were obscured by the glare of the headlights.

It wasn't until I heard a familiar voice that I recognized them.

"Damien, Brian, are you boys in here?"

In a way, I was somewhat relieved—yet slightly annoyed—that they'd managed to find us. I knew I was probably in trouble again.

"Yeah, Pat, over here—but be careful, there's a hole to the left side."

"Damien, where's Brian?"

"He fell through the hole in the floor that leads to the basement."

"Crap, is he alright?"

"Yeah, he just twisted his ankle a bit."

"We'll find a way down."

I peered into the other room, finding a kitchen or what was left of it at least. I showed Pat and Steven to the door to the basement, and we very carefully went down some wooden stairs until we reached Brian. Helping him to his feet, we settled him onto some crates. Pat examined his ankle, wrapping it and fashioning a splint from the available wood. Afterwards, he turned to me and simply shook his head.

Before he could speak I asked, "Pat, how did you find us?"

"We went to Mr. Craft's office, where he found an old map that showed this house. We came home to get you, but it appears that you beat us to the punch. Steven touched the table and glimpsed what you boys had been planning to do, so we made our way here. You should have waited for us."

"We couldn't just stay home and do nothing. Oh wait, do you hear that sound?"

We all heard the sound of the girl crying echoing through the basement with increasing clarity. Our attention was drawn to a gaping hole on the opposite wall, from which a light was getting intensely brighter by the moment. Gradually, the figures of the couple stood in the opening, gesturing for us to follow them. It seemed we had stumbled upon what we were looking for.

I was more than a little anxious, but at the same time felt exhilarated and curious about our two glowing friends. I slowly approached, extending my hand towards them. The young man reciprocated with a faint smile. As my hand passed through his, I could feel a tingling energy surging through my fingertips.

It was clear just how sad they were, and ready for it all to be over.

Chapter Eleven: Pat.
Light at the end of a tunnel.

I gasped as Damien approached the two apparitions. It was rare for me to have the opportunity to witness spirits like those my brother could see—each time it occurred, it left me breathless.

Initially my first instinct was to stop Damien, but as I observed their interaction with each other, I knew he was safe. As Damien and the young couple lingered, waiting for us to follow, I recognized the need for us to move on. The main issue at hand was what to do with Brian. It was clear that he was going to have some difficulty walking. Upon surveying the basement, I noticed numerous items still stored in crates and boxes. Despite the extensive damage caused by the fire upstairs, most of the belongings that were stored in the basement remained in good shape. Among the items, I spotted some antique furniture by the staircase. There was an old hand-carved headboard that caught my eye. As I pushed it aside, I spotted a pair of old crutches in the corner. Although they were pretty weathered, they appeared to still be sturdy enough.

I handed them to Brian and asked, "Do you think you can make it?"

He rose from his seat and steadied himself with the crutches before shifting his weight onto his foot, taking a step forward. "I might be a little slow, but I think I'll be alright."

I turned to Damien and said, "Please help Brian if he needs your help. Let's see where this leads—hopefully we can uncover the whereabouts of their remains."

We followed the young couple into a series of tunnels beneath the mansion, leading to an ancient sewer system that had clearly been abandoned for years. Tree roots had penetrated the slimy walls, winding their way through the passages. A damp, decaying odor permeated the air, while water still flooded sections of the floor, and we were greeted by the occasional sights and sounds of rats that had taken up residence down here. Damien assisted Brian from slipping on the slippery, mucky floor. As long as we kept up with the apparitions, we didn't need our flashlights, as their glow illuminated the tunnel, guiding our path.

We followed the ghosts down many passages until we stumbled upon another concealed tunnel within a wall, seemingly leading out of the sewer system. The network of tunnels resembled a labyrinth. It would be so easy for someone to get lost down here if it weren't for our ghosts guiding us. I sensed that we were getting closer to their bodies as we ventured deeper into the tunnels, and had a sneaking suspicion that we might not be alone. I quietly cautioned the others to keep an eye out.

We arrived at a junction within the complex labyrinth of passages. The ethereal glow emanating from the ghosts got even brighter, revealing a crypt beneath the cemetery just past the estate. The scent of death remained in the chamber. Damien and Brian gagged in disgust as they stepped into the room, and I instructed them to stay back for the time being. Upon glancing upwards, we were met with the sight of numerous coffins protruding out from the walls and the ceiling. The roots of the trees were tightly wrapped around them, firmly anchoring them into place as they had done for years. Some had crashed to the ground, their caskets shattered open, with ancient bones scattered around them.

At the base of a flight of stone steps lay the decomposing remains of the young couple. The two ghosts were huddled together, embracing each other on the stairs beside their lifeless forms. The girl continued to weep. Steven approached to examine their remains, removing his gloves and showing a slight tremor in his hand. Turning away in disgust, he slowly touched the deceased young man. My heart ached for Steven, knowing the emotional toll these experiences took on him.

Approaching the deceased couple, I reassured them that we would take care of everything and that they could rest now. The young man looked up with a gentle smile, then gracefully rose, taking his girlfriend's hand as they made their way towards the exit. With a final wave, they vanished beyond the confines of the crypt. Following their departure, we now had to depend on the flashlight. I followed, attempting to open the massive solid wooden door, yet it wouldn't budge. Gesturing for Damien's assistance, we positioned Brian on an old coffin for him to rest. Damien and I exerted pressure, causing the wood to creak under the strain. Just as we were making progress, I heard Brian call for Damien.

We all turned around, and in the darkness, a multitude of eyes emerged from the expansive tunnels that led to unknown destinations. The eyes flickered in the beams of our flashlights, resembling those of wild animals. As they drew closer, Damien and I exerted all our strength and the door finally yielded. Steven rushed to assist Brian, and together we made our escape. Glancing back into the room with my flashlight, I witnessed a horde of vampires emerging from the tunnels, pursuing us relentlessly. We had become their hunted prey.

We slammed the door behind us, utilizing two grand marble planters on each side of the door to strengthen it. Damien and I positioned the planters to obstruct the entrance, although we knew it would only be a temporary obstacle. Exiting the old mausoleum led us to the heart of the oldest part of the cemetery. Our primary objective was to get back to the mansion and reach the car, but we knew we needed something to defend ourselves when the vampires confronted us. I was concerned that Brian's injured ankle might slow our progress, but to my relief, he produced a small amount of pixie dust from his pocket. Although only a fraction remained due to a spill during his fall, it proved invaluable. While we all couldn't fly out of here, it did grant Brian an edge in case the pursuing vampires closed in on us.

It seemed the vampires back at the crypt were fledglings, lacking the strength to take flight. Hastening our pace, we could hear the vampires breaking through the door, followed by the sound of a loud crash. As we neared the iron gates leading out of the graveyard, it seemed our escape was within reach. However, a few vampires managed to slip past us, obstructing the exit and forcing us to confront them in combat.

Chapter Twelve: Damien.
Out of the fire into the cemetery.

It seemed that we were cut off from leaving. I thought if I could apprehend just one of the vampires, I would be able to siphon off their remaining life force. Pat and the others were equipped with weapons capable of taking out a vampire, so we weren't going down without a fight. Unfortunately, Brian lost some of the pixie dust when he fell through the floor of the house—otherwise, we could have just flown out of there and returned in the morning to retrieve the bodies of the young couple.

I knew Pat was right in suggesting we wait, yet my impatience prevailed as usual. I couldn't sit around and do nothing. It was now my responsibility to find a way to free ourselves from this predicament. By my estimation, there were approximately ten vampires surrounding us. All I needed to do was get a hold of one or two of them, then I would be able to turn this around. The situation called for me having to bring out my fangs and claws.

As I extended my razor-sharp talons, I prepared for the upcoming battle dance I had engaged in previously with the red-haired vampire. Pat, Steven, and Brian unveiled an array of holy water, crucifixes, and even a crossbow. I wondered where Pat had concealed that crossbow on his body—he was always one to anticipate every possible scenario. As we drew closer to the gates, the vampires obstructed our path without advancing themselves. What were they waiting for? Was this what Pat would call a standoff? For the moment, they still maintained the advantage. Were they exercising caution, apprehensive of what I did to the other vampire? They simply stood there, hissing at us. Regardless, I had to get us past that gate. However, as I started to go for it, a mist began to blanket the ground of the cemetery. Now what was going on? Whatever it was, the vampires seemed equally displeased by it too.

The mist began to swirl around the tombstone, and specters emerged from all corners of the cemetery. One by one, the apparitions commenced their assault, whisking away the vampires. Was this the spirits' way of seeking retribution for the vampires' killing the kids? Not one to overlook an unexpected opportunity, I seized the moment and went for one of the vampires. Despite Pat's warning to stop and wait, it was too late—I was heading right for one of the vampires near the gate. It noticed me and was starting to approach as well. Just as we were about to engage each other in combat, we both were blindsided by something that knocked us right off our feet.

I slid across the ground and collided with a majestic tombstone adorned with the face of an angel gazing down upon me. Brian swooped down and got me to my feet. I lost sight of what happened to the other vampire. Then, as I turned around, the mysterious figure in the hooded cloak was standing at the entrance of the gate. It seemed was way stronger than the other vampires who had now returned to its side. Even the ghost's efforts to fight it off had little effect, as they were merely brushed aside. Realizing that I wasn't strong enough to take on whatever this was, I knew this could be bad for all of us. However, the hooded figure lifted a bony hand, commanding us to stop and not harm the fledglings.

I approached Pat, massaging my shoulder after the impact with the ground.

Pat lowered the crossbow and advanced a step. "We have no intention of hurting anyone. Our sole purpose is to leave tonight and return tomorrow morning to properly attend to the remains of the young couple. They deserve to be respectfully taken care of."

The creature lowered its hood, revealing a monstrous visage unlike any other vampire. More bestial in nature, its skin was gray and adorned with deep wrinkles. Its ears, large and pointed, added to its menacing appearance. The nose, flattened and angled upwards, gave it a fierce countenance. Rows of razor-sharp teeth lined its mouth, yet its most chilling feature was its eyes, which gleamed in a luminous yellow hue. I didn't know about everyone else, but I felt more than a little uneasy and compelled to look away. The sight before me was unlike anything I had ever seen before, but I recalled vampires fitting this description in one of Pat's books back home. While I couldn't remember the specific term they used for them, there was a particular characteristic about them I found interesting.

I took a step forward. "You're a female."

Pat grabbed my arm. "Damien, don't be rude."

"I'm sorry, I don't mean any disrespect. Our intention isn't to hurt anyone, but I thought your species were all male. We were wondering who you are, and what you want with us?"

The demon grinned. "My name is Belladonna, and I am of the Nosferatu lineage. While our kind is predominantly male, there are a few of us who are female. I also oversee these orphaned fledgling vampires. Their makers met their demise in a clash between two rival clans, one of which your parents belonged to."

Maybe this demon had the answers that I'd been looking for.

"Who are you, and what do you know about my family?"

"In response to your initial inquiry, the Nosferatu are the primordial and oldest of the vampires, distinct from those who once walked as humans. We cannot assume a human form—we perpetually dwell in the shadows to evade detection by those who denounce us as creatures of the night. Furthermore, we've bestowed the gift of vampirism upon select human beings, sparing those who we did not exterminate or feed upon, thus creating the second generation of our kind.

"On your second point, my knowledge of you and your family is rather limited. The information pertaining to you is shrouded by powerful magic and securely sealed away. What I am aware of dates back to a significant conflict that transpired over a century ago between Countess Báthory and Count Orlok, sparking a fierce war between their respective clans. Throughout the years, a few vampeal offspring have come into existence. While the Countess accepted them, Count Orlok harbored deep apprehensions regarding their potential as tools of destruction against other vampires. He deemed them abominations and said they should be put to death. The conflict claimed numerous lives on both sides, leaving behind these fledglings who lost their sires. They pose no threat to you; their presence was merely out of curiosity and vigilance."

"Then why did the red-headed vampire attack me and come after us?"

"That was Val—he struggled to come to terms with the loss of his sire. Their bond was exceptionally strong—not unlike the connection between you and your flying companion over there. It's now clear to me why he is so special. Val found it extremely challenging to rein in his bloodlust. We are strictly forbidden to kill the ones we feed on, but as you can see with the young couple, he wasn't doing well. You just happened to come along at the wrong moment."

Pat came and positioned himself next to me. "May I ask why you're stopping us now—why not just simply grant us permission to proceed?"

"Because we needed to talk. You may depart and return tomorrow to recover the bodies. The individual who was responsible for their deaths has faced the consequences—thus, I implore you to refrain from troubling my children and vow to exert my utmost effort in ensuring their compliance. As much as I can keep any child under control, of course."

Pat glanced in my direction. "I'm certain that the Society will concur, under the condition that such an occurrence is never repeated."

"Then we've reached a mutual agreement."

The Nosferatu and the other vampires stepped aside and graciously opened the gate to allow our safe passage. The mist and the apparitions had now receded into the peaceful slumber of the cemetery, leaving me to ponder their promise in hopeful anticipation.

Chapter Thirteen: Pat.
Job well done.

Steven and I entered Mr. Craft's office and found him seated behind his desk.

"Gentlemen, please come in and take a seat. I wish to express my gratitude for your exceptional work. The remains of the young couple have been recovered, and their families have been notified, allowing them closure. Hopefully, Belladonna will be able to maintain order among the remaining young vampires. This hasn't been the first time that one of the vampires has gone rogue, and it probably won't be the last, given the challenge of managing a supernatural child. We shall continue to monitor the situation closely. I know you've tried to shield Damien from these affairs, but he is proving to be a promising amateur detective. Your collaborative efforts are commendable. It's a shame that Brian will soon be leaving, but I'm confident that your paths will cross again in the future."

"Could you provide further insight into what happened to Damien's family?"

Mr. Craft shook his head, furrowing his brow. "I regret to say that it's above even my pay grade. Belladonna's observation regarding the ongoing conflict between the two clans is indeed accurate, though. We were instructed to keep Damien hidden and safe until he became ready."

"Ready for what?"

"I don't know."

We were all startled as a familiar voice came from the dimly lit corner on the opposite end of the office. I couldn't help but smile as Tillis, the pigeon lady, took a seat across from Mr. Craft. She was a figure etched in my memory from the day Damien came into our life. Tillis, an elderly woman of African descent, who wore her hair in black and gray dreadlocks that fell over a vibrant floral dress, initially appeared to me as a kind and helpful elderly lady. However, as time went on, I came to realize that she was way more than that.

"I beg your pardon, gentlemen, but I couldn't help but put my two cents in. I must admit that the intricate details surrounding Damien's family remain a mystery to me. At least, who his parents were. I was entrusted with the task of keeping him safe because he's just one piece of a larger puzzle."

I snickered softly as I recalled the stories she shared with me when we met, and I was delighted to listen to her once again. "It's truly a pleasure to see you again and hear what you have to say."

"Mr. Davidson remains as courteous as ever, I see. Allow me to tell you that many others are destined to cross paths with you and Damien—their paths will intertwine like the threads in a finely woven piece of fabric, coming in and out of your lives for a very long time."

"Tillis, are you implying that our destinies are linked?"

"Yes and no, my dear young man—the trajectory of one's journey is not always a linear one, influenced by the choices they make and the paths they decide to embark on. However, for certain individuals, their paths may cross multiple times, regardless of the route they choose to follow."

I gave her a curious look. "So, you possess the ability to see the future?"

"No, not particularly, but I acquired a valuable little trick from my daughters a lifetime ago. I possess the ability to perceive the auras that surround an individual, and I can see the interconnecting threads that bind us together in this lifetime and the next. Just as you and Detective Miller will have ample opportunities to work together in the future. Let me demonstrate, Mr. Davidson. Take my hand, close your eyes, and now, open them."

I held the old woman's hand and did as she asked. When I opened my eyes, I was overwhelmed by the colors from our auras and strands that connected us together.

I released Tillis' hands and asked, "Does this resemble what my brother sees?"

"In part—he lacks the strength to perceive the connections to the living at this moment, but in time, he will. Here I am, rambling on again. You don't need to listen to a long-winded old lady."

"Not at all, it's a pleasure."

"Aww, you're too kind. Mr. Craft, do you have anything to add?"

"No, I believe that should suffice. I'll keep you updated with any further developments."

"Thank you, Mr. Craft. It was a pleasure to see you again, Tillis."

Steven and I bid farewell and departed. I asked Steven if he wanted to have dinner before heading back to Dayton later. He agreed, and we decided on Chinese, so I took him to my favorite restaurant called the Pink Buddha, which was owned by friends Ray and Craig. I loved their exquisite dim sum menu, which they introduced us to many years ago during our college days. We indulged in some of our favorite dishes including succulent pork buns, savory pot stickers, and flavorful spare ribs.

I was delighted that Steven had returned, and it had been a pleasure to work with him once again. However, one challenge we faced in our relationship was the difficulty I had in concealing my thoughts or emotions from him. Despite his efforts to control it, there were moments when things just slipped out.

Steven giggled. "What are you thinking about?"

"Oh, not much—just reminiscing about the past."

"Pat, you know that the boys believe we... did something last night."

"I know—let them think what they want to, and perhaps they'll leave me alone about meeting someone."

"You know it wouldn't be bad if we did do something—but at the moment, I'm just getting out of a bad relationship, and so I'm not quite ready."

"Given all my responsibilities at home and work, I'm not either. But if you wanted to come visit again..."

"I'm sure I'll be back this way, and if you happen to be in Dayton, you should definitely stop by. How do you think Damien will react to Brian's leaving?"

"It will hurt for a while, but I'm sure he'll bounce back eventually. The challenge lies in the fact that he is special, just like us. It's not going to make things easier for him to find someone. I hoped we could find out more about the mystery surrounding his parents, though."

"I'm confident he'll find out who he is before too long. Though I'm sad I won't get to witness Brian's transformation firsthand, unfortunately, I should really be getting back."

We settled our bill at the restaurant, and I walked Steven out to his car. I gave him a warm hug and bid him a fond farewell before he drove off into the night.

263

Chapter Fourteen: Damien
We all have to grow up sometime.

Well, the countdown begins. Brian will be turning eighteen and has to go back to Neverland. I know how hard it'll be to say goodbye and how strange it'll feel to live my life without him. It seems like only yesterday when he came through the door of that foster home, before I was kicked out for kissing him. I was so angry about it at the time, but looking back on it now, it's just something I had to go through. If I hadn't, I probably wouldn't have been in a relationship with Brian for the past few years, nor would I have ended up living with Pat and Matt.

Still, it doesn't make all this hurt any less. I tried to maintain a strong façade for as long as possible; I've worn this mask so long, what difference does once more make? I just have to remember not to let Brian see me cry.

Yesterday, we celebrated Brian's birthday early and gave him a farewell party with Pat, Matt, and the other members of the foster home, giving us the opportunity to spend the day by ourselves. If it were within my power, I would freeze this moment forever. Since this was our final evening together, we decided to spend it together in the barn where our journey as a couple began. We'd made it our special place. Pat promised to keep Matt away so we could have our privacy.

I looked over at Brian while we were lying back in the loft, both naked, for what seemed like an eternity. I admired his magnificent body as I traced the outlines of his chest and abdomen, progressing down toward his intimate regions. We were still sweaty from making love repeatedly for the past few hours. I anticipated that both of us would be sore for the next few days. I noticed strands of hay protruding from various parts of our bodies and, with a gentle smile, I delicately removed a few from his hair.

Brian said, "You have that faraway look again. How are you doing?"

"Okay, given the circumstances. This is the last time we'll be together like this. I'm going to miss you so much. You kind of became an addiction that I can't resist."

"I've cherished these past few years with you, Damien. You've been my first boyfriend, and how grateful I am for that. From the moment I stepped into the Crabtree house and caught you peeking out of the upstairs bedroom, I knew that you were the one I wanted."

"Still, you were pretty lucky I decided to forgive you for not supporting me when Miss Crabtree caught us kissing. That incident got me kicked out of the house. In spite of it, I'm grateful that you were my first too."

"Everything worked out in the end. You now have a permanent home with Matt and Pat, or until you find someone you want to be with and share your life with, which I'm confident you will. Just don't be afraid to embrace your emotions again."

"Easier said than done. Remember I have a little secret that I can't just tell anyone about. Especially now we know there are people watching me. I was hoping the Nosferatu could have told me more about my family and the fledgling vampires that she is watching over. I guess Pat, Matt, and I will need to embark on a journey to discover the truth for ourselves."

"I wish I could help. However, if I hear anything that might be useful, I will be sure you find out. I promise to come back to see you next year to see how you're doing. Always remember that you hold a special place in my heart, regardless of where I am."

"What are your plans upon your return to Neverland?"

"My sister and I have established a university on the island of Elsewhere, where other Lost Boys like me have lingered too long in Neverland. They can't return to their former lives in this realm, but they have the opportunity to mature and evolve into their true selves."

"Sounds great—I wish I could be there with you."

"Me too, my love—but the one thing I've learned from Pan is that life is a big adventure; you just have to let yourself live it. Sometimes the end of something is just a beginning for something new."

"You know, Brian, I think you've been hanging around Pat too long. He's beginning to rub off on you."

"That might be true—just don't let Matt's influence start to rub off too much on you."

We both laughed hysterically, and I slid my arms around him in a tight embrace, clinging to him with all my might. Suddenly, Brian sat up, groaning, doubled over in agony.

I grabbed his arm gently. "Are you alright, Brian?"

He winced as the transformation had started. I swiftly rose and hurried to the entrance of the loft, calling out for Pat and Matt to come quickly. Hastily I grabbed my robe, wrapping it around me, and it felt as though we were all scurrying about as if preparing for a newborn baby. I asked Pat what was going on, and why Brian was in so much pain.

"Damien, have you heard of someone experiencing growing pains? Brian is undergoing such a phenomenon, but at an accelerated rate. He's aging rapidly, transitioning in a matter of minutes, hours… honestly, I don't really know."

"Is there anything we can do to help?"

"No, we must be patient and allow the process to run its course."

We tried to make Brian comfortable as much as we could. His temperature was alarmingly high, causing his body to feel as though it was on fire. Then, after a grueling thirty minutes, Brian managed to rise to his feet, finding relief after the pain had stopped. The formerly lanky teenage boy had turned into a muscular jock. I grabbed Brian's robe—not that I was complaining about seeing my soon-to-be ex-boyfriend in all his glory. He appeared slightly younger than Matt and Pat, a fact I would have found unbelievable had I not witnessed his transformation firsthand. I gently wrapped the robe around his body, and hugged him tight.

"Brian, are you alright?"

He stepped forward and stumbled, but I managed to steady him. Brian's breathing was heavy and wheezy, yet he mustered the strength to say, "I'm feeling a bit disoriented; I need to adjust to my new body. How do I look?"

"You're not going to get any complaints out of me."

"Well, if you could help me to the house, I ought to freshen up. I should be going soon. I don't know how long it'll be before I start growing again. I'll have my family pick up my things in a few days, and there are a few things I've left behind for you guys to remember me by."

I released a deep sigh as we made our way back to the house. Brian tidied up and gathered his belongings, bidding farewell to Pat and Matt with warm embraces before turning to me. Despite my efforts to hold back my tears, my composure failed. It took both Pat and Matt to gently separate us. With a serene smile, Brian sprinkled himself with pixie dust and gracefully ascended into the air.

"Damien, you've always been my happy thought, and my utmost joy."

Before I could process it, he had disappeared into the night sky. I turned to Pat at last, releasing all the emotions that had been building up inside me. He embraced me before returning to the house.

For a while, all I wanted to do was sleep and curl up and cry. I was merely going through the motions of my daily existence, but gradually, I emerged from that dark place as I eased into a new routine.

I've been casually dating, but it's been challenging to find someone I can trust with my little secret. In the meantime, I've been keeping busy assisting Pat and Matt with various cases when I'm not doing stuff for school. However, I still look into the sky now and then, waiting for Brian's return.

The end

Epilogue Damien
Open a new door

It was the weekend before Halloween, and Pat and Matt had decided to take a little road trip up to Dayton.

They planned to spend a few hours with Steven before heading over to a dance club known as 1470 West. They've been trying to lift my spirits and get me out of my funk, as I had been feeling rather moody ever since Brian's last visit a few months ago. I thought I'd moved on, and although I've dated a few guys, it just hadn't worked out. Initially, we would get along fine, but every time I felt I could trust someone with my secret of being a vampeal, the relationship just didn't work out for various reasons.

Sometimes I found myself wondering whether the red-headed vampire was right. Is it conceivable for someone to love me despite my secret? Would Brian have loved me if he wasn't special himself, being one of the Lost Boys from Neverland? I was beginning to wonder if I might have been better off being like Matt, not really getting too attached to anyone.

It was truly painful when I had to say goodbye to Brian, even though it was expected. Now that he'd found a new boyfriend, I was torn between feeling joy for his discovery of love and being envious—wondering if it was ever going to work out for me, especially given how things have been for Pat and Matt. Both are great guys, and they both deserve to be with someone and not tied down with me. Tonight, they were diligently working on a case to apprehend a serial killer targeting gay men at rest stops. I was so grateful for the opportunity to help out more ever since I graduated from high school.

This evening, Pat and I are planning to go to a gay dance club, which will be a nice change from the bars and clubs in this area. Meanwhile Matt and Steven plan to stake out the rest areas with Matt's trucker friends. Now, the only thing I can do is figure out what to wear. After trying on various outfits without success, I finally settled on my red jeans and a white shirt with puffy sleeves. Admiring my reflection in the mirror, I couldn't help but appreciate how I looked. Though I might not find someone I could connect with on as deep a level as I did with Brian, there's nothing stopping me from finding a charming companion for the evening.

Pat cleared his throat upon entering the room. "Damien, if you've finished admiring yourself in the mirror, we should get going."

I chuckled. "Okay Pops, let me get my stuff, and I'll be down in a moment."

I retrieved my wallet and keys before meeting Pat and Matt downstairs.

Matt greeted me with a whistle. "It seems as though somebody's trying to get lucky."

Again, I chuckled. "Well, you never know—it doesn't hurt to be prepared."

Pat interjected, "Indeed, but you still have to be careful—we still don't know who the perpetrator behind the murders at the rest stops is."

I turned to Pat and said, "Could you and Matt just ask the ghost who killed them?"

"All the victims' spirits could recall were blurry faces and red eyes, indicating a definite supernatural origin. Their life force had been completely drained from their bodies, leaving them mummified without the bandages."

"That's a hell of a way to go. I promise I'll be careful."

We all got into the truck and made a brief stop to drop off Matt at one of the rest stops, for him to meet Steven and his friends.

Upon arriving at 1470 West, we entered the establishment where the doorman checked our IDs. Following the check, we were each issued colored wristbands—Pat received a green one and mine was red, indicating that I was eighteen and thus only allowed to drink beer and wine. The club was a spacious venue, featuring pool tables on the left, a bar on the right, and a dancefloor in front shaped like a plus sign.

Above, a large disco ball hung from the ceiling, casting mesmerizing lights in every direction. Tables were strategically placed around the dancefloor and its surroundings. We secured a table near the rear bar, situated next to a stage likely reserved for drag performances.

Pat got some kind of cocktail and kindly brought me a beer. As we settled in, observing the lively dance floor, I couldn't help but notice the distinct groups gathering at various sections of the bar, depending on what you're into. The dance floor was predominantly occupied by lively twinks, and the opposite corner housed a gathering of ladies. Among the diverse groups, my attention was turned to a young guy dancing with a lesbian who could have been his older sister. He was slender, likely around my age, with short, spiky blond hair. He couldn't have been much taller than five feet six inches, and was dressed in gray parachute pants adorned with numerous zippers running down the legs, paired with a matching jacket.

As he shifted, I caught a glimpse of his black t-shirt. I got a sense I knew him from somewhere before, but I struggled to pinpoint his identity. Suddenly, a surge of energy coursed through me, leaving me feeling slightly strange. That was interesting; I felt compelled to observe this young man more closely. I told Pat I'd be back, and proceeded to stroll around the dancefloor, my gaze fixed on the mystery man. I observed him intently until the crowd dispersed and he stood there, pausing and turning, looking right at me for a brief moment. He smiled and the crowd enclosed him once more. I swiftly went back to the table.

I must have had a strange expression on my face, because Pat asked me, "Damien, are you alright? You look like you saw a ghost."

"No, I think that's more your area of interest—but have you noticed the young blond guy over there next to the older lady that looks like she could be his sister?"

"Yeah, what about him?"

"For some reason, I feel that I've met him before, but I can't think from where."

"Now that I think of it, he does look a little familiar. If you like him, go over and say hi."

"I don't know, I shouldn't really get involved. You know I can't tell people about what I am."

"Without sounding too much like my brother, you don't have to marry the guy! Just go over and ask him to dance. We have a few hours, so go have fun. Still, you probably shouldn't go home with him tonight anyway, especially considering the current situation with the serial killer."

I sighed. "I know."

"If you won't, let me go over on your behalf. I'm tired of you moping around the house—you need to have some fun!"

Then, before I could object, Pat was off. However, before reaching the guy, the lady rose and intercepted him, positioning herself in front of the young man. She proceeded to interrogate Pat thoroughly.

I snickered as Pat stepped back, trying to calm the lady and explain the situation to them both. They all turned toward me, and I felt like I was caught doing something wrong. I was more than a little embarrassed at that moment. Then, before long, Pat and the young guy had returned to our table.

Pat introduced the young guy as Jason, and we settled at a bigger table where we all ordered glasses of white wine. I shook his hand and introduced myself. As we talked, Jason told me they were from Dayton and that the lady with him was his boss and good friend. After taking a few sips of wine, we got up and danced for a while.

I don't know what it was, but I really felt like I was starting to like this guy. After we exhausted ourselves from dancing, we returned to our seats and finished our drinks. I reached for his hand, and we shared a few affectionate kisses. Just when we were becoming better acquainted, Pat mentioned that it was time to go as it was a long ride home, and he needed to get up early. Upon learning that Pat was a truck driver, a look of astonishment appeared on Jason's face.

"Have you heard about the killings?" he asked.

Pat glanced in my direction. I responded, "Yeah, Pat's among the truck drivers who discovered the most recent victim. They're keeping an eye out in the area to see if they can catch the guy."

"Damien," Jason said, "can I have your phone number? I'd really like to see you again if you like—maybe we can talk some more?"

I graciously agreed, and we exchanged phone numbers. I embraced him warmly and gave him one last kiss, before Pat gently reminded us it really was time to go. Jason returned to his friends, and I just smiled as we walked away. I glanced back one last time, and caught Jason returning the smile right back at me.

Pat placed his hand gently on my shoulder. "Perhaps now you can move on from Brian."

I turned to him and smiled. "Brian who?"

The story continues in Skeletons in the Closet…

Also by the Author

Skeletons In The Closet

So what's a young gay boy from the suburbs of Dayton, Ohio to do when he comes out to his family, only to find out his family has been keeping their own secrets?

Jason Wynwood just turned 18 and found out he is in a long bloodline of witches. As Jason searches for love, he falls for a mysterious black-haired gentleman named Damien.

Jason is thrown into a dangerous world of magic with witches, vampires, and werewolves, and a glittery nightlife of sexual pleasures.

He also discovers that young gay men have been turning up dead at rest stops all over the surrounding areas. Police suspect that it's the work of a serial killer.

But when a friend ends up dead, it becomes personal. Can Jason find the killer before anyone else turns up dead?

In The Light Of The Moon

You can't keep running from your past, especially when it has four legs and fangs.

In the exciting second installment of Tales of a Gay Witch, we return to Jason and his friends six months later as they are coming to terms with the events of last year.

Jason thought he could move on with his life after Damien left in search of information about his mother, after finding out she might be alive after all, but is struggling to adjust to life without him.

He is persuaded to go out and meet up with his friends at his favorite night club 1470 West, where he meets a handsome young man named Mickey. That same night, Jason is informed by Detective Miller, now a good friend of his, to be on the lookout for Jo's ex-husband Rex, who might be coming their way. There have been a number of sexual assaults and murders targeting young lesbian women up in northern Ohio, and Rex is suspected of being involved. Jo's ex-husband was always a nasty, abusive piece of work, but to make things worse, Rex is a werewolf and an alpha to boot.

It's up to Jason to rally his friends again; he is tasked with protecting the people he cares about before it's too late.

Curious Thing About The Apartment Vent

Just because you're alone, doesn't mean someone doesn't know your business...

Lucas, the closeted son of a preacher who just graduated from Florida Atlantic University, returns home and is forced to make a life-changing decision--can he live a lie and marry his lifelong BFF, who his overbearing parents have been plotting to matchmake him with for years? Or, will he stay in Florida and start a new, more open life that he knows they will never approve of?

Tyler, a talented artist on the edge of seventeen, is about to finish high school, and is looking forward to becoming a proper adult and fully exploring his sexuality. However, he soon discovers there's a kink in his plans--his father has decided to rent out the studio apartment he's been living in, putting an end to the independence he's enjoyed until now.

Lucas answers an advertisement for the apartment, and sparks fly from the very first moment the boys meet--though both are reluctant to explore things further, since it wasn't what either of them had planned for their futures.

But sometimes life isn't that simple and doesn't always go exactly as planned...

About the author

R.D. Noland was born in the suburbs of Dayton, Ohio. During his last two years of high school, he attended M.C.J.S. studying art, photography, and printing. He took some classes at the Sinclair Community College to continue his education.

He was raised by his mother, grandmother and aunt, all of whom shaped the way he viewed the world.

Mr. Noland moved to Florida in 1989 with his significant other and their two cats. They closed the chapter on that relationship after many years and sadly the cats went with his ex. Later he adopted two dogs that he fell in love with; they became his baby girls.

He was accepted by some major art schools but could not afford to attend, so he enrolled in a local college to study art. He has worked as a custom picture framer and a freelance artist in several galleries and frame shops.

Mr. Noland feels at his best when he is creating, so please join him on this new creative adventure and see where his imagination takes us.

Notes

Notes

www.ingramcontent.com/pod-product-compliance
Lightning Source LLC
LaVergne TN
LVHW021241141224
799129LV00001B/30